P9-EEJ-388

COUNTRY
LEGACY

THE MAVERICK'S CHRISTMAS TO REMEMBER

Christy Jeffries

Special thanks and acknowledgment are given to
Christy Jeffries for her contribution to the
Montana Mavericks: The Lonelyhearts Ranch continuity.

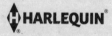

Recycling programs
for this product may
not exist in your area.

ISBN-13: 978-1-335-52350-1

The Maverick's Christmas to Remember
First published in 2018. This edition published in 2022.
Copyright © 2018 by Harlequin Enterprises ULC

For questions and comments about the quality of this book,
please contact us at CustomerService@Harlequin.com.

Harlequin Enterprises ULC
22 Adelaide St. West, 41st Floor
Toronto, Ontario M5H 4E3, Canada
www.Harlequin.com

Printed in U.S.A.

Christy Jeffries graduated from the University of California, Irvine, with a degree in criminology and received her Juris Doctor from California Western School of Law. But drafting court documents and working in law enforcement was merely an apprenticeship for her current career in the dynamic field of mommyhood and romance writing. She lives in Southern California with her patient husband, two energetic sons and one sassy grandmother. Follow her online at christyjeffries.com.

To Kate Gove Campbell, one of my favorite people on earth and a member of my Golden Girls. You are always the first to order my books, the first to respond to my texts and posts, and the first to laugh at my dumb jokes. Even from across the country, your support is always constant. Not only do you give the best and tightest hugs, you have taught me how to be a better friend and you make the world a warmer and happier place. You are the Rose to my Dorothy, and I can't wait to share a lanai with you...

Chapter 1

Caroline Ruth loved romance and happily-ever-after stories and all sorts of things that her academic-minded mother considered nonsense. That was how she knew with absolute conviction that this career as an assistant wedding planner in Rust Creek Falls, Montana, was tailor-made for her. And so did her boss, who was currently on her honeymoon and had left their newest client in Caroline's more-than-capable hands.

Josselyn Weaver sat across the desk from her, poring over bridal gown catalogs as they both waited for the groom to arrive to the couple's initial consultation. Picking a gown always seemed to hold the most excitement for the brides, but Caroline knew that booking a venue was the foundation of building a successful event. After all, the guest list and decorations and theme usually depended on the location.

Caroline's stomach growled and she wished she had stopped for a breakfast croissant at Daisy's Donuts on her way to work this morning. But she'd been so eager to get to the office and prepare for this meeting that she'd barely allowed herself time for a couple of bites of a disgusting protein bar she'd found smashed in the bottom of her giant tote bag.

"So when we met a couple of months ago, you were pretty adamant that you wouldn't be getting married anytime soon," she finally said when Josselyn looked up from a glossy magazine spread. Not that she wanted to rush the bride, but Caroline had too much energy for long periods of silence, no matter how comfortable they were. Besides, the more she could learn about the couple she was working with the better. "I'm glad to see you changed your mind."

"I know. I remember you telling me that

you'd be planning my wedding soon and I thought it was the craziest thing I'd ever heard." Josselyn's eyes were bright with humor, and Caroline smiled since she was well accustomed to people not really taking her instincts seriously. The bride continued, "I'd just moved to Rust Creek Falls to take the school librarian job and wasn't even looking for a date, let alone a relationship. I know people say that love finds you when you're not looking for it, but if someone had told me that I'd be engaged by Christmas, I never would have believed it."

Caroline gulped as a shiver made its way down her back.

Engaged by Christmas.

The words brought back the memory of Winona Cobbs's prediction that Caroline would be engaged before she turned twenty-four. That was a bit more than a month away, which meant that if the old psychic was correct, the right man would need to come along soon.

Shaking off the tingling vibration along her skin, Caroline glanced down at the wastebasket by her feet and wondered if she'd been a little too quick to throw out the half-eaten protein bar. She was suddenly feeling a bit light-headed and needed to keep this meeting moving along.

"So tell me about your fiancé," she suggested. She was almost as new to the small town as Josselyn was, and despite the fact that she'd already assisted with a few weddings out at Sunshine Farm, Caroline hadn't met the groom yet.

"Drew is an obstetrician at the Rust Creek Falls Clinic. His first wife died in a car accident several years ago, and since this is his second wedding, I want to make sure that I'm being respectful to her memory."

"Of course." Caroline nodded sympathetically. "And if I remember correctly, he also has an adorable son that introduced you two, right? I'm guessing you'd like him to be involved in the wedding somehow."

"That would be wonderful," Josselyn replied as her cell phone vibrated. She looked at her screen. "Drew just texted. Apparently, he ran into his brother at Daisy's, but the good news is that he's bringing donuts to apologize for running late."

"No problem." Caroline waved a hand in dismissal as her stomach clenched in anticipation of a sugary treat. Josselyn picked up another bridal gown magazine, and Caroline decided to steer her toward the more important decisions. "Have you guys talked about the size of the wedding or whether you want it to be indoors or outdoors?"

"Well, he's originally from Thunder Canyon, so we were kind of thinking something in Kalispell might be a bit more accommodating for everyone traveling. I'm not really sure how many people we're inviting, but his family is huge. And I was hoping we could set the date within the next couple of months, so we would probably need an indoor venue since Montana winters can be pretty unpredictable."

"I know the perfect place!" Caroline jumped up so quickly she hit her knee on the corner of the desk drawer. "Hold on, I have more information on it in one of these binders."

Their current office building used to be an old train depot at Sawmill Station, and when her boss, Vivienne, converted it for her wedding planning business, her husband had built her a wall of bookshelves. Cole had promised to install a rolling ladder when they returned from their honeymoon, but until then, Caroline had to drag a piece of furniture over and climb up on it every time she needed to reach something on the top shelf.

To take her mind off the fact that she was balancing on an antique wooden chair in a pair of high heels, Caroline kept talking, hoping her enthusiasm disguised her nervous energy. "There's a historical brick building in Kalispell that is currently an art museum, but the back opens up into this huge open space. And get this. It used to be a Carnegie library before the city relocated the library to their current location. But the historical society rents it out for events and, well, if I wasn't so short I could reach the brochure and just show you."

"Can I help?" Josselyn asked, coming to stand nearby.

"Nope, I almost have it." It wasn't very ladylike—especially in an above-the-knee ruffled skirt—but Caroline put one foot onto a shelf to shimmy up just a little higher and stretched her arm as far as it would go until her fingers could grasp the bottom of the binder. As luck would have it, that was the exact moment when the front door opened.

"Drew…!" Josselyn said, her voice trailing

off as she obviously walked away from the bookshelves and toward the entrance. Caroline would've stayed focused on what she was doing, but then the bride added, "I didn't know you were bringing Ben and Craig with you."

Caroline turned in surprise at the mention of unexpected people and brought her foot off the shelf a little too quickly. There were three men standing in the entryway. However, she only had eyes for the one carrying the pink bakery box. He was wearing a tan Stetson with a red plaid shirt, but that kind of standard cowboy attire was a dime a dozen around this town. What made her dizzy with excitement was the hook-shaped scar on the right side of his neck…just like the man Winona Cobbs had predicted.

Biting her lip, Caroline blinked in wonder at the new arrival. This was it. He was here. She just knew it.

Overwhelmed, underfed and perhaps a bit too eager, Caroline rocked the chair as she tried to climb down. Unfortunately, her high heel hooked onto one of the narrow armrests and she went down fast. The last thought to go through her mind was *Engaged by Christmas*.

* * *

Craig Clifton saw the woman fall as if it was happening in slow motion. Dropping the box of donuts, he sprinted toward her just as he heard the deafening *thunk* of her forehead bouncing off one of the wooden shelves. Still a couple of feet away, Craig dived at her in a last-ditch effort to brace her landing. But the odd angle and the impact of her deadweight knocked them both to the ground.

Luckily, he was able to pivot his torso at the last minute, and the back of the lady's head, as well as her shoulders, landed on his abdomen instead of the hardwood floor. Craig had absorbed most of the impact, but they were now sprawled out in the shape of a T and his childhood friend was yelling at them to stay still.

"Don't move her," Drew ordered as he knelt by Craig's hip. Catching his breath, which had been knocked out of him when they'd collided, Craig sucked in a gulp of air and saw the woman's long brown hair rise and fall with his chest.

"I can barely move myself," Craig replied, lifting a hand to the bump rising along the back of his scalp, not surprised to find his

Stetson missing. His brothers referred to it as his "going to town hat" since he tended to wear it whenever he left the ranch. Craig wiggled his toes inside his boots and relaxed when he was confident that all his appendages were in working order.

"She's unconscious," Drew continued as he touched the lady's neck, probably checking for a pulse or a broken bone or whatever else it was that doctors checked for. Then Drew looked over to his brother, who was also a physician and currently crouched down with his hands on his knees, staring at the unresponsive woman instead of asking how his best friend's spine was. "Ben, I left my bag in my car back at Daisy's. Do you have yours in the truck?"

"I'm on my way," Ben replied.

"Should we call an ambulance for her?" Josselyn asked as she stood over all of them, concern etched on her forehead.

"It would probably take too long for one to drive here from Kalispell," Drew replied. "Her heartbeat and breathing seem to be stable and I'm not feeling anything broken. But judging by how hard she hit that shelf on the way down, I wouldn't be surprised if she has a concussion."

"That was my first thought," Ben said as he returned with his doctor bag. "We could take her to the clinic in town, but she's going to need a CT scan and would have to go to the hospital in Kalispell for that anyway. If we're going to drive her anywhere, it should be there."

"Wouldn't it be dangerous to move her?" Josselyn asked her fiancé, and Craig found himself thinking the same thing.

"Well, we can't leave her on top of Craig forever, as much as he might enjoy that." Ben smirked, then must've noticed the concern on his soon-to-be sister-in-law's face. "I promise she'll be fine."

Craig had grown up with the Stricklands and knew that if Ben could make jokes during a time like this, the situation couldn't be entirely dire. He forced his muscles to relax and wondered how he'd gotten roped into accompanying two of his best friends over here for a wedding planning appointment of all things.

One minute he'd been in line at Daisy's Donuts with Ben, discussing leasing fees for bulls, and the next, Drew was taking them both over to the new ranch at Sawmill Station to get a look at the latest herd of longhorns the Daltons were selling. Apparently, it just so happened that the wedding planner's office was located on the same property.

"I'm fine, by the way," Craig said, since nobody seemed to be concerned about his health after he'd taken a dive like that. He looked across the floor to where the pink bakery box had opened and spilled out its contents all over the wooden planks. "But since I'm stuck down here, can someone hand me a donut?"

"If you're healthy enough to complain, you're healthy enough to wait your turn." Drew's eyes flickered briefly over Craig before he slipped a Velcro cuff onto the arm of the unconscious woman, whose head was still propped up just below Craig's chest. "Besides, I've seen you take worse falls off a bucking horse back in the day. Now, hold still while I get her blood pressure."

"But he's not a young buck anymore," Ben said, wiggling his eyebrows with humor and making Craig feel every one of his thirty-five years. The hard floor underneath him and the odd angle of his body weren't helping the uncomfortable stiffness settling over him.

"I could still outride you," Craig challenged. "Unless you're getting in a lot of saddle time in between shifts at that fancy hospital of yours in Billings."

"Possibly," Ben said, passing him a glazed twist that had landed halfway on top of a piece of wax paper. "I haven't seen you move that fast since Brown Fury slammed you up against the pen in the midstate finals."

"That bull was one mean son of a—"

"Should I call someone?" Josselyn asked, interrupting Craig's reminiscing about his rodeo days. But it was either talk about something else to get his mind off the injured woman currently on top of him or lie here thinking about the last time he'd been powerless to help a different injured woman.

"She's stable," Drew responded. "But we should get her to the hospital in Kalispell to have some tests run."

Having grown up on his family's ranch in Thunder Canyon, Craig was no stranger to small towns and medical emergencies. The people there were used to taking care of their own. Not that this particular lady was his own. Hell, he didn't even know this woman resting so peacefully against him, the porcelain-white skin of her cheek relaxed against the red plaid checks in his shirt. But if the doctors said they could drive her from Rust Creek Falls into Kalispell, then that was what they would do.

As Drew and Ben gently lifted her off him, Craig left his uneaten donut on the floor and rose to his feet, tamping down his impulse to scoop the woman into his arms and carry her himself. After all, he was the one who'd saved her from a second blow to her head when he'd landed underneath her. That kind of bond made a man feel a certain responsibility. But Ben already had her off the ground, with Drew stabilizing her head as they walked toward the door. Which was probably for the best considering they were both trained in moving patients, whereas Craig was better trained to haul her around like a bale of hay.

"I'll grab her purse," Josselyn said as everyone seemed to spring into action.

Craig had barely enough time to scoop up his fallen hat and make it outside to open the back door of his crew cab truck. He quickly hopped up and slid across the seat to help gently maneuver the unconscious woman inside. He found himself with her head resting on him again, but at least this time it was on his lap as he sat upright on the bench seat. If he'd wanted to badly enough, he probably could've switched spots and let Drew sit back here with her. However, Craig had already taken on the rescue role inside the office and he didn't feel right about abandoning the poor lady now.

He had to shift his hips carefully in order to fish the truck keys out of his front pocket and pass them to Josselyn, who volunteered to drive so that Drew could be available to check the woman's vitals during the twenty-five-minute drive. Ben, realizing that there wasn't enough room in the truck, decided to drive Josselyn's car back to Sunshine Farm.

"Who should I notify?" Ben asked, and all eyes turned to Josselyn.

"Um, she works for Vivienne Shuster, but Viv and Cole Dalton are in Fiji on their honeymoon. Like me, she's new to Rust Creek Falls, so I'm not really sure who she'd want me to call locally. I think her parents are college professors or something but I don't know where they live."

It seemed so intimate to be talking about the personal details of a woman he'd never met. A woman whose brown hair fell in soft waves against the denim of his jeans. Craig cleared his throat. "What's her name?"

"Caroline Ruth," Josselyn said, then put the truck into gear.

Caroline.

Her body was slender and petite, but she had curves in all the right places. A rush of shame filled him as he realized he was blatantly staring at an unconscious lady. An unconscious and vulnerable lady with a body encased in delicate, clingy feminine fabric that would never suit life on a ranch. Not that Caroline looked like the type to spend much time working in the outdoors. He narrowed his gaze toward her high-heeled sandals and the bright pink polish on her toes. She never would've fallen off that chair if she'd been wearing sturdy boots and functional jeans. But she was a wedding planner, so what did she know about physical labor?

Josselyn took a bend in the two-lane highway a bit too sharply and Craig instinctively wrapped his hand around Caroline's waist to make sure she didn't accidentally tumble off the seat. The touch sent an electric vibration up his arm, making him feel like even more of a creep, so he yanked his hand away quickly, but didn't know where to put it. Lifting his elbow to the top of the backrest, Craig studied her face for signs of pain or discomfort. Fortunately, she appeared to be completely relaxed in her unconscious state, almost as though she were blissfully at peace.

Caroline Ruth was definitely an attractive woman, he'd give her that. Still. He was in no position to be noticing such things, and she was clearly in no position to be receiving his unwanted attention. Craig shifted guiltily in his seat and Caroline's eyes suddenly shot open.

"Hey there," Craig offered weakly. What else was he supposed to say to a complete stranger with her head in his lap? Caroline smiled dreamily at him before her lids fluttered closed and she was out cold again.

Chapter 2

Caroline heard steady beeping before feeling something squeeze around her upper arm. It took considerable effort to raise her eyelids, and when she finally got them to stay open, there were a few seconds of blurriness.

Where was she?

What had happened?

"She's awake," a woman said, and Caroline blinked several times until the light fixture in the middle of the white ceiling came into focus. She wiggled her toes as her hands flexed against something that felt like a starched sheet. Was she in a bed? She was definitely lying down.

"Caroline?" someone else asked and she turned toward the voice, her eyes narrowing on the person standing beside her. A woman with steel-gray curls and smooth skin the color of dark copper placed a calming hand on Caroline's shoulder. "Can you hear me?"

"Where am I?" Caroline asked.

"You're in the emergency room at Kalispell Regional. I'm Dr. Robinson. Do you remember what happened?"

Caroline shook her head and then flinched at the stabbing pain that shot through her forehead.

"Careful, now," the doctor continued. "From what I understand, you hit your head pretty hard. Your friends brought you in and we did an MRI while you were still unconscious. We think you have a concussion, but we'd like to get a CT scan of your brain to rule out anything more serious."

"My friends?" Caroline asked, then turned toward the other woman in the room. She sighed when she saw Josselyn Weaver on the other side of her bed.

"Hey, Caroline." Josselyn squeezed Caroline's hand, accidentally dislodging some little white wires and causing a shrill beep.

"Don't worry. It's just the oxygen reader," the doctor offered, putting the plastic device back over Caroline's pointer finger. "You up for answering some questions?"

"Sure," Caroline said as she tried to sit up. She was relieved that the rest of her body cooperated and that her head was the only thing hurting.

"Do you know your name?" Dr. Robinson asked.

"Caroline Ruth."

"And what day is it?"

She blinked a couple of times until it came back to her. "November 21."

"Good." The doctor's bright white smile was reassuring. "And what did you have for breakfast today?"

Caroline's stomach rumbled at the reminder. "Only a couple of bites of a protein bar. I should've gotten a breakfast sandwich at Daisy's this morning but I didn't want to be late for my appointment."

"Oh? What kind of appointment?"

"I'm a wedding planner."

The physician looked over to Josselyn, who

nodded in agreement. The questions must be part of some kind of test and Caroline hoped she was passing.

Dr. Robinson lifted a finger in front of Caroline's nose. "Do you know where you live?"

Caroline's eyes followed the finger as she rattled off the address for the tiny guest house she'd rented in the heart of Rust Creek Falls several months ago. The sooner she answered everything and proved she was perfectly fine, the sooner she could get something to eat.

"What's the last thing you remember before coming to the hospital?"

"I was talking to Josselyn about her wedding and I climbed up on a chair to get the binder with a brochure for a venue when..." Caroline trailed off as she couldn't recall what had occurred after that. Lifting her fingers to stroke her forehead, she asked, "Is that how I fell?"

"Yes," Josselyn said, sighing as though she'd been holding her breath up until this point. "You went face-first into one of the shelves on your way down and were out cold. We didn't want to wait for an ambulance, so we brought you straight to the ER."

"We?" Caroline asked and looked around the room. There was another man near the partitioned curtain of the exam room, but he'd been talking to a nurse outside and she'd assumed he was another doctor.

"That's—" Josselyn started, but Dr. Robinson cut her off.

"Do you know the name of this man?"

"No idea," Caroline replied, hoping her honesty wouldn't mean that she couldn't get a snack soon. When she'd been ten years old, her dad had to be rushed to the hospital near the faculty housing at Berkeley. He'd insisted that it was only heartburn and asked Caroline to go to the cafeteria and get him some vanilla soft serve to soothe the acid. Turned out it was a perforated gallbladder and because he'd eaten the ice cream, the anesthesiologist delayed the surgery until his stomach was empty. It had been a long ten hours of her dad doing his awful Oliver Twist impression by begging for more food and insisting he was starving.

"Technically, she hadn't met me prior to her fall." The man the doctor had just asked about stepped forward and placed an arm around Josselyn's waist. "I'm Drew Strickland, by the way. You're planning our wedding. We had just walked in the door and you'd turned to look at us. That's when you got your foot twisted in the chair and fell."

"We?" Caroline asked again, feeling like a parrot. Her eyelids were getting heavy again and all she wanted was a hot breakfast sandwich and a nap. "Who's we?"

"Me and—" Drew was cut off by Dr. Robinson holding up a hand like a stop sign.

"Do you remember them walking in the door before you fell?" the emergency room physician asked.

Caroline focused on a bright red electric outlet on the wall in an effort to concentrate, trying to form an image in her mind. But nothing was coming to her. She replayed the events of the morning over and over again, and the weight of the silence in the room suggested that everyone else knew what two plus two equaled and were desperately waiting for her to shout out, "Four!"

However, she was drawing a complete blank. In fact, she was positive that there wasn't anything else that happened after that. She was getting tired again, probably from concentrating so hard, and just wanted to fall asleep.

Couldn't they simply tell her what had happened and let her take a nap?

"Sorry, I don't." Caroline shrugged, then yawned. "The last thing I remember was reaching for that binder on the top shelf."

It was then that a second man walked into the room and Caroline's breath caught as he took off his cowboy hat and ran a golden hand through his black, close-cropped hair.

Her entire body eased back onto the bed and she smiled in relief, everything finally making sense. "Oh, there you are."

"So you know him?" the doctor asked, jerking a thumb to the newcomer.

"Of course," Caroline said, then blinked slowly as the pillow cradled her head. "That's my fiancé."

Her fiancé?

Craig's head whipped around to the hallway behind him. But nobody else was there. He opened his mouth to tell the doctor that he'd never even met this woman, but nothing came out. The air had been sucked out of his lungs, and probably out of the entire room, judging by the equally confused expressions on everyone else's faces.

Caroline's head injury must be more serious than they'd originally thought if she was babbling incoherent randomness. Scratch that. Her statement had been clear and articulate, but it made absolutely no sense. Nor did the way she was looking at him, her doe-shaped brown eyes all dreamy and her wide lips parted in a hazy smile as though he was the only one in the room, or at least the only person who mattered. It was the same look Tina had given him before she'd died, and the comparison made his blood go cold.

Caroline looked nothing like his high school sweetheart, but Craig's memory had already been triggered, and that rush of helplessness filled his veins the same way it had all those years ago when they'd been trapped on the highway, waiting for the rescue workers to pry them out of the wreckage. He would've looked to Drew or Josselyn for an answer, but he couldn't tear his gaze away from Caroline.

Logically, he knew he wasn't reliving that awful night nearly fifteen years ago, but when Caroline's eyes finally drifted closed, Craig raced to her bedside and grabbed her hand as though he alone could will her back to consciousness.

"She'll be fine," the ER doctor told him with a gentle pat on the shoulder, a move likely designed to reassure loved ones. No doubt, it had worked for the doc countless times in the past. The only difference in this situation was that Craig didn't know the current patient, let alone love her.

"But I'm not—" Craig started and Dr. Robinson interrupted him.

"Let's step into the hallway where we can talk." The physician's reassuring pat turned into a firm nudge as she steered him toward the nurses' station.

Craig turned back toward his friends, who were slowly following them. Josselyn's mouth was slightly open and there were a few squiggly creases between her eyebrows while Drew simply stared in concern as though Craig had been the one to hit his head and get the sense knocked out of him.

Not that Craig could blame the guy. There might be plenty of reasons why Caroline accidentally called him her fiancé, but there was absolutely no explanation for his intense emotional reaction to someone who was a total stranger.

While it was already embarrassing that the

others saw him respond like that, it would be even more confusing and downright mortifying to explain what prompted him to run to her side and clutch her hand as though she was dying.

Despite the couple approaching, Dr. Robinson faced Craig and directed most of the information his way. Something about a concussion and needing consent for a CT scan to rule out any long-term damage. "My recommendation is to run a few more tests and then have her stay overnight for observation. Does your fiancée have any other family members we should notify or can you authorize consent?"

"She's not my fiancée." The words finally tumbled out of Craig's mouth in a rush as he tugged on the collar of his work shirt. "In fact, I've never met her before."

"Well, she certainly lit up when you came in the room," Dr. Robinson replied, one hand on her hip as though she wasn't buying Craig's version of the situation. "I didn't even need to shine my light in her eyes when I was examining her because her pupils contracted and focused on you like you were the be-all and end-all."

"I promise I've never seen her before today. Right?" Craig shot a pleading look toward Drew for confirmation. "I have no idea why she would think we knew each other, let alone that we're engaged. Maybe I resemble her real fiancé and the concussion just has her brain rattled?"

"I'm pretty sure she's single." Josselyn finally spoke up and Craig felt the oxygen slowly return to his lungs. "We've only talked a handful of times, but she's never mentioned a significant other. Plus, she doesn't have an engagement ring."

At first Craig was filled with a sort of vindication from the proof that he wasn't her fiancé. However, that was soon replaced by utter bafflement. "Then why would she imagine herself being in a serious relationship at all?"

"Maybe she has amnesia?" Josselyn suggested.

"I suppose that's possible." Drew turned down one corner of his mouth, his expression suggesting that it wasn't possible at all. "However, she had full recollection of all the events leading up to her fall."

"It could be confabulation." Dr. Robinson

now spoke to Drew, her voice lowered as she threw out phrases such as *memory production* and *cognitive distortion* and something else Craig couldn't quite make out.

"Hmm." Drew nodded. "I've read case studies, but have never seen it manifested in a patient."

Craig rolled his eyes. "Do you think you guys could use some layman terms for us nondoctors?"

"Confabulation is similar to amnesia in that it's a memory disturbance. It can happen when there is some type of damage to the brain. Caroline seems to remember almost everything leading up to her injury, but to fill in the gaps on what she doesn't know, her mind has invented a story to explain it."

Oh, boy. He should've stayed in Thunder Canyon this week. Pinching the bridge of his nose, Craig asked, "But why would she need to make up a lie about being engaged?"

"It's not a lie." Dr. Robinson shook her head. "To her, it's very real."

"Okay, so then we just tell her that she doesn't know me and that she doesn't have a fiancé and she's good to go." He slapped his palms together as though it were that simple. And it would've been if Craig had been speaking to the vet out on the ranch. Cows and horses never had issues like this.

Dr. Robinson shared another look with Drew before answering. "In theory, we would always recommend telling a patient the truth. But in this case, she hit her forehead, where the frontal lobe is encased, and that makes it hard for her to retrieve and evaluate memories. So in instances of confabulation, it doesn't matter what you say. Her brain is in a fragile state right now and will only be able to understand what her frontal lobe is telling her."

"How long does this last?" Craig folded his arms across his chest and looked longingly toward the ER exit doors. "I mean, do I actually have to pretend to be her fiancé?"

"I'm sure Dr. Robinson doesn't want you to pretend to be anything," Drew offered, looking at his watch.

"No, of course not. I'm simply recommending that we don't upset the patient until all the tests come back and we know more about what's going on."

"So when will that happen?"

"As soon as her fiancé gives us consent?"

"But I'm not—"

Dr. Robinson held up her palm. "I was kidding. When she wakes up again, we can get her verbal consent. But is there anybody else we should notify in the meantime? Anyone else who can give us a better medical history?"

All eyes turned toward Josselyn again. "I looked through her purse, but I couldn't find her cell phone. I heard back from Vivienne earlier, and she confirmed that Caroline's parents are out of the country right now on some sort of teaching sabbatical and she doesn't remember her mentioning any friends or family nearby. I would hate to leave her here all alone. What if she wakes up and is confused again?"

"Obviously, we can't leave her here alone," Craig said.

Drew looked at his watch a second time. "I have to get back to Rust Creek Falls before my son gets out of school."

"I'd stay, but I have to speak at the city council meeting this evening to ask for extra funding for the elementary school library. If I miss it, I'll have to wait another month to get my proposal approved."

"Maybe I'll call Ben and ask…" Drew started.

"No way," Craig said, shaking his head before his friend could even finish the thought. "I can stick around."

Chapter 3

The words had flown out of Craig's mouth before they'd had a chance to logically form in his brain. Not because his skin itched with jealousy at the mention of another man staying with Caroline when she was this vulnerable, but because Craig hadn't been able to shake this sense of responsibility for her since he'd seen her slipping off that chair. If he tried to explain this impulse, it wouldn't make sense to his friends. Hell, it didn't even make sense to him.

"I mean, if I'm her... I...uh...mean...if Caroline thinks I'm her fiancé, then obviously she'll be expecting me to be here when she wakes up. I wouldn't want to make things worse. And it's not like it's a big deal," Craig added, more for his own benefit than to convince his friends. "I'm not really doing anything else today."

It was true. The late fall season was the slowest time on his family's ranch because they'd already sent their latest herds to market and didn't plan to start breeding the new calves until after the new year. He was in Rust Creek Falls to visit two of his brothers and to check in with some of the other local ranchers for what his dad referred to as "old-fashioned market research."

Josselyn frowned. "I'm not sure if it would be in Caroline's best interest to let her continue thinking that you two are really engaged. After all, she'll get her memory back eventually, won't she?"

Dr. Robinson lifted her shoulders in a shrug. "Like I said, we'll know more after her tests. I'd feel better holding off on any treatment plan or official diagnosis just yet, but if it *is* confabulation strictly caused by a brain injury and not caused by a mental health issue or dementia, then this memory setback likely won't last too long. With all that being said, while I wouldn't advocate lying to a patient, I don't necessarily see any harm in letting them believe in whatever is going to give them a sense of peace for the time being. Our biggest goal right now is to keep Caroline as calm and relaxed as possible."

Drew looked at his watch again. "Are you sure you want to stay, Craig?"

"I don't *want* to," Craig clarified, more for himself than for anyone else listening. "But if it's the easiest solution and it will keep Caroline calm so that she can heal, then I'll do it."

There, that sounded plausible enough, even to his own ears. After several more rounds of "Are you sure?" followed by Craig's growing insistence, he eventually found himself sitting on the miserable plastic chair beside her bed in the exam room, drinking cold coffee and scrolling on his smartphone for the latest feed and grain reports. It wasn't the same as getting out to the other ranches and talking directly to his fellow cattlemen, but he couldn't just blow off all his work duties to sit around playing nurse.

Normally, he rarely used the device except for making calls and often told his brothers that any cattleman worth his salt didn't rely on fancy gadgets that could easily get busted working on the ranch. If Craig was in the field and needed information off the internet, he usually just asked his brother Rob or waited until he could use the computer at the house. However, now that their father had been bitten with the technology bug and insisted on sending group texts with links to online articles, Craig found himself a reluctant user.

"Do you think I could have one of your Life Savers?" Caroline's soft voice was so unexpected that Craig dropped his phone, its reinforced hard-shell case preventing the screen from cracking on the tile floor.

"Huh?" Craig asked, then wanted to kick himself for sounding like such a dope.

"One of your Life Savers." Caroline pointed to the front pocket of his shirt, where he always stashed a roll of his favorite cherry-flavored candy.

His chin dropped toward the empty pocket. Okay, now that was weird. He'd had less than half a roll when he'd left his brother's house this morning and then had nervously plowed through the rest of them by the time Caroline had undergone her MRI. Since she'd never been conscious during any of the times he'd popped one into his mouth, there was no way for her to be aware of his little sugar habit.

"How do you know about my Life Savers?" he asked, trying his best not to completely disregard the doctor's instructions about keeping Caroline calm.

"You always have them," she replied, her smile all dreamy again and his insides responding the same way they had the last time she'd woken up and grinned at him. "Plus, you smell like cherries."

Craig let out the breath he'd been holding, mildly relieved with the second part of her explanation. "Do you know who I am?"

Caroline's smooth forehead pinched into several lines as she studied him. Thinking that maybe she'd lost a pair of glasses in the fall and couldn't see his face clearly, Craig leaned closer as intense concentration took over her expression. She opened her pouty bow-shaped lips several times before defeat filled her eyes. "I don't know why I can't think of your name."

"It's Craig," he replied, wanting to pump his fist in celebration. Not that he should be basking in her confusion, but if she didn't know his name, then she'd finally realized that he was actually a complete stranger. That meant that her amnesia spell or confabulation—or whatever it was—had finally passed and she no longer needed him to take care of her. He extended his hand as he introduced himself. "I'm Craig Clifton."

Caroline inhaled deeply through her nose as she nodded. But instead of taking his proffered handshake, she laced her fingers through his. "Of course you are. I must've hit my head pretty hard to forget my own fiancé's name."

Poor Craig looked about as confused as Caroline felt. It must be difficult for him to see the woman he loved like this. But then again, at least he wasn't the one who'd completely forgotten most of the specifics about the person he was supposed to be marrying. Hopefully, it wasn't a bad omen for their relationship if she could perfectly recall every other detail of her life except for the one that was arguably the most important.

She squeezed her eyes closed as though it might help paint a more accurate picture of the man in her mind. Caroline remembered

the hook-shaped scar on his neck, she remembered he liked cherry-flavored candy and...
And that was where all the details stopped.

"Are you in pain?" Craig asked. "Should I call for a nurse?"

"Oh, no." Caroline's lids popped open. "I was just trying really hard to recall something more concrete about us, like how long we've been together or where we first met or where you live and work. But I'm drawing a complete blank, and to be honest, it's making me a little nervous."

"Don't be nervous," he said quickly, then rolled his lips inward, causing him look like a child who was trying to bite back a secret. The expression didn't exactly alleviate her fears. Her growing anxiety must have been obvious because he added, "The doctor said that when you hit your head, it might have caused a few problems with your memory."

Panic clawed at her throat, and she could feel the cold, dry air hitting her eyes as they grew wider than normal. "Like amnesia?"

"Not exactly." Craig rubbed the scarred area of his neck. "The doctor called it something else, but it's similar. She can probably explain it to you way better than I can."

Craig stood up, and his cowboy boots clicked against the floor as he strode over to the open curtain and waved down a hospital employee in surgical scrubs. Caroline couldn't hear what he was saying, but his thumb gestured her way and her gaze traveled from his hand down his tan, muscular forearms to where his red plaid work shirt was rolled to the elbows. Because of the way he was standing, Caroline could only study him from a side angle, but as she took in his well-rounded shoulders and flat abs and long, strong legs encased in faded denim, she couldn't help but wonder how in the world she could possibly have forgotten a perfect form like his.

When he pivoted to walk back toward Caroline, her tummy dropped and she got lightheaded again. The view from the front was just as good as the one from the side. Heat flooded her cheeks and she asked, "Do you think I could possibly have a drink of water?"

"I asked the doctor about you being able to eat or drink when you woke up and she said only a sip of water until after your CT scan. She doesn't anticipate you needing any sort of surgery, but they haven't ruled it out yet."

The mention of surgery should've had her concerned. Instead, a sense of relief blossomed inside her chest. It was reassuring that her fiancé knew her well enough to understand that she'd be worried about eating and drinking and obviously had taken steps to provide answers for her. Maybe she'd even told him the story about her dad's gallbladder surgery and the soft-serve ice cream. It was crazy to think that this man beside her was probably privy to all of her secrets and all of her needs. Now if only she could recall some of *his* preferences—besides candy, obviously—then they'd be on equal footing.

Craig picked up a water bottle from the bedside tray table and unscrewed the plastic cap before gently holding it to her lips. "Not too much, now."

As she drank, she made the mistake of lifting her eyes to his face and was hit with such an intense attraction that she swallowed way too quickly and began coughing. Craig used the back of his hand to wipe the water that had dribbled down her chin. It was such an intimate gesture, not necessarily in a sexual way but in the way someone would take care of a loved one.

Something warm spread through Caroline's body. She was loved. By this man. While the feeling wasn't entirely familiar to her, it was certainly exciting. And very welcome. After all, Caroline had known that she wanted to be a wife and a mother since kindergarten, when she and five-year-old Scott Sullivan had staged a mock wedding during recess. Unfortunately, they'd barely gotten through the first-grade minister's line of "You may kiss the bride," before the teacher had put a stop to things and called Caroline's and Scott's parents to inform them that students needed to keep their hands—and their lips—to themselves at school. When her mother asked why she'd wanted to marry Scott Sullivan, Caroline had told her that he was the only boy who wasn't playing handball that day. After that, Rita Rodriguez, department chair for Women and Gender Studies at Wellesley College, had made her daughter promise that she would never settle for a man.

And Caroline never did again. In fact, she hadn't so much as had a boyfriend because every guy she'd ever gone out with hadn't felt like "the one."

So, while she couldn't remember a thing

about the handsomely rugged cowboy before her, Caroline had every confidence that she belonged with him. Unlike her recess-length courtship with the first available kindergartner, there was a powerful emotional connection between Caroline and Craig. Because of her absent memory, she didn't understand it right that second but she felt it deep in her core. In twenty-three years, her instincts had never led her astray, and even her normally evidence-based mother had to admit that when Caroline felt something, she really felt it. In fact, after her college graduation, Caroline's father had given her a framed quote by Charles Dickens that read "A loving heart is the truest wisdom."

Her mother hated that quote.

Luckily, her parents were currently in India, her mom conducting research on the history and success of matriarchal tribes as her father compiled literary works by the lesser-known authors of the British colonies. Which meant they were too far away to question her every decision.

"How's everyone feeling in here?" Dr. Robinson asked, sliding back the partition.

Craig immediately stood up, because of

course, he would. As if Caroline would ever pick a guy who wasn't a complete gentleman at all times. However, his current white-knuckle grip on the bedside rail suggested his good manners were also helping to mask his discomfort and the nervous way his eyes were looking everywhere but at her.

"I'm still a little fuzzy on some things," Caroline replied before reaching out the hand not connected to the oxygen wires and placing it over Craig's. His fingers were warm, his skin slightly rough and very bronzed—probably from working outside or wherever it was that he worked. Caroline would worry about remembering those kinds of details later. She didn't want to make her fiancé feel awkward or unimportant. That was why her smile wasn't forced when she added, "But I'm content and comfortable for now."

Dr. Robinson nodded before looking away, lines scrunching across her otherwise smooth brow. Caroline followed the woman's gaze in time to see Craig give a brief shake of his head.

They were obviously referring to the fact that she hadn't fully regained her memory and Caroline wanted to kick her feet in frustration like a petulant child. But her legs were tucked in under a weight of blankets, reminding her of the utter lack of power she had over both her mind and body. "So when can I go home?"

"Well, the radiology tech is on his way now. After the CT scan, we'd like you to stay the night so we can keep an eye on your concussion. As long as all the tests come back negative, I don't see any reason why you couldn't go home tomorrow."

Caroline didn't even realize she was now clutching Craig's hand until his fingers slid through hers and squeezed with reassurance. "I've never stayed the night in a hospital before."

"Nothing to worry about." Dr. Robinson tsk-tsked, reminding Caroline of her Nan, who made that sound anytime she thought her granddaughter was too skinny and not eating enough. The physician nodded toward Craig. "And your man here said he plans to stay the night with you. So between him and all our nurses, you'll never be alone."

"You're going to stay?" Caroline smiled at Craig and his eyes seemed to turn a darker shade of blue.

He cleared his throat and focused on the blood pressure machine beeping behind her. "Um, if that would make you feel more comfortable. Sure."

If she had the full use of her faculties, Caroline would probably be able to better guess at what the man was thinking. However, she had absolutely no clue what her fiancé's normal response would be in a situation like this. Did he really want to stay? Or was he just being polite? Judging by the forced expression on his face, Caroline would assume the latter. But before she could let him off the hook, the tech showed up to take her for the CT scan.

As the hospital employee maneuvered her hospital bed through the corridors, Craig walked beside Caroline, her bright pink tote bag looped over one of his broad shoulders. She recognized the purse as the one she'd picked out this morning to go with her new heels and had to swallow a giggle at how much it clashed with his red plaid shirt.

But when it got caught in the elevator door behind him, Caroline could no longer hold in her laughter. "Do you always carry my purse for me?"

He gave a slight grunt, then hefted it higher

onto his shoulder. "It was either this or leave it behind in the exam room where anyone could walk by and steal it."

After the radiology tech helped her transfer off the bed and onto the cold platform for her scan, he asked her a series of questions, like whether she was wearing any jewelry or had any metal implants anywhere in her body. Then the tech asked the one question that really threw her. "Any possibility that you're pregnant?"

Caroline's lungs seized and her mouth froze into a circle, unsure of what the answer was. Surely she would remember something like that, wouldn't she? She was only twenty-three years old and had been waiting to have sex until she'd found "the one," which she'd obviously found. She turned pleading eyes to Craig, hating that she couldn't even recall if they'd had intercourse before, let alone whether they'd used any form of birth control. "Have we... I mean is there...?"

She couldn't finish the embarrassing question with the radiology guy looking on, his clipboard not even raised high enough to cover his curious smirk.

A rosy shade of pink stole along Craig's

hardened jawline and his eyes went wide, probably as he realized that he was the only person in the room who could possibly answer such an intimate thing.

"Uh…" His mouth opened and closed several times before he finally cleared his throat. "I think they did a blood test in the ER before the MRI. Maybe it says in her chart or something?"

"Let me take a look," the tech said before flipping a few pages. Caroline wanted to yell at the man for not bothering to check her file first. But she was too busy forcing her muscles to relax against the narrow sheet-covered table underneath her. "Nope, no baby on board. We're good to go."

Caroline almost sighed out loud as the air finally left her chest in a whoosh. Not because she didn't want to have a baby—she most definitely wanted to be a mother someday. She just wanted to fully remember the man who could possibly be the father of her child. Unfortunately, the more she tried to drag the information from her brain, the more her head pounded.

The tech raised and lowered the table and gave her some final instructions about remaining still. At some point, the room went darker, but Caroline's breathing remained ragged and her thoughts kept spinning.

While knowing that she wasn't pregnant gave her one less thing to worry about in the overall scheme of things, it didn't stop her from craving more details about the man she was planning to marry. And what their current physical relationship was like.

Watching Craig's retreating form as he exited the room, she came to the pulse-elevating realization that just because she couldn't remember having sex with him didn't mean she couldn't vividly imagine it.

Chapter 4

Man, Craig had dodged a serious bullet back there in the radiology room when Caroline looked at him with those doe-shaped brown eyes and wanted to know if they'd ever had sex. How in the hell was he supposed to know the answer to that? Okay, so obviously he knew the actual answer, but he'd been clueless on how to phrase it out loud.

She'd fallen asleep again during the procedure, but Dr. Robinson assured him that it was pretty normal for a concussed patient to doze off occasionally and that resting could actually help her brain heal. As long as Caroline's pupils weren't dilated and she could hold a conversation when she was awake, she was supposedly fine.

By the time they finally got her admitted and assigned to a room, it was getting close to dinnertime and Craig was starving. When she'd confessed that she'd never stayed overnight in a hospital, she'd looked so scared, so frail.

The main goal was to keep her from getting stressed or putting any more strain on her traumatized brain. However, in order to keep his wits about him and do that, he also needed to eat something. Although, what kind of fake fiancé would he be if he sneaked off while she was sleeping to go down to the cafeteria to get some dinner?

Looking around for a pad of paper so he could leave a note, his eyes landed on her ridiculously huge purse sitting in the corner of the room. He had saddlebags smaller than that thing and never understood why some women insisted on hauling everything they owned all around town with them. If he were a betting man, he'd place odds that she had plenty of paper and at least several pens in the thing. The problem was, there was no way to look inside without feeling like he was invading her privacy.

Rubbing a hand through his close-cropped hair, he asked himself for the thousandth time today, "How in the hell did you get yourself into this situation?"

"What was that?" Caroline's sleepy voice was deep and husky, a stark contrast to her delicate and feminine looks. It was also as arousing as anything he'd ever heard before.

"I was just wondering where I could find a pen and paper."

Her sigh came from the back of her throat. "I always carry some in my purse."

"Yeah, I assumed as much but it didn't seem right snooping through your things when you're sound asleep."

"It wouldn't be considered snooping since I don't have any secrets from you." Clearly, her mind was way too fragile to grasp the magnitude of just how many secrets they actually had since they didn't know the first thing about each other. When he didn't respond, she continued, "Are you always this proper around me?"

"I…uh… I guess I'm just a proper type of guy." Or a guy who was simply way out of his element.

She studied him in the dim glow of the room, the sun fading outside the window. He rocked back on his boot heels and looked over his shoulder at the door. They should probably keep that open so nobody got the wrong idea about what was going on in this private room. And since when did hospitals have private rooms?

When Craig had surgery after his second clavicle fracture, he'd been stuck in traction next to an old man who used to confuse the emergency call button for the television remote. The volume on the evening news would go up every time the man didn't get his bedpan in time. If Caroline had a roommate like that, Craig wouldn't have to worry about that electric current charging through his body every time she turned those pretty eyes his way.

"Why did you need paper and a pen?" Caroline asked, and Craig turned back to her.

"Oh. I thought about grabbing a bite to eat downstairs and wanted to leave you a note in case you woke up and I wasn't here."

"So, you're both proper *and* thoughtful." Her full lips turned up at the corners, but her questioning gaze remained steadily fixed on him, as though she were awaiting more discoveries about him. "I'm starving."

"The doctor cleared you to eat after she got the radiology report and there was nothing to indicate you needed immediate surgery. They delivered a tray for you earlier," he said, wheeling the small table over to her bed. "I think it's meat loaf."

She lifted a plastic cover off the plate and crinkled her pert little nose at the cold gray lump underneath. "I'm missing part of my memory, not my taste buds. Since you're going to the cafeteria, would you mind bringing me something from there instead?"

"Sure." He replaced the lid and moved the offending plate out of the way. "What do you want?"

"Anything. Surprise me."

Crap. He'd walked right into that trap. Craig eyed her small frame and couldn't even begin to guess what kind of food she ate. Obviously, it wasn't his preferred meal of steak and potatoes because she looked like a strong wind would blow her away before the next winter storm. For all he knew, she was one of those women who constantly monitored every calorie in order to keep her waist so tiny.

"Maybe a salad?" he suggested because he got the impression that she didn't maintain her lithe shape by being a hearty eater.

"Ugh, no." Caroline stuck out her tongue and made a gagging sound. "I hate vegetables. Except for french fries."

"I don't think french fries count as a vegetable."

"They're from potatoes, right?" Caroline's voice held a trace of laughter.

"Fine. I'll get you some french fries. How about a double bacon cheeseburger to go with that?" he offered, trying to match her playful tone but sounding more facetious.

"Mmm. That sounds perfect," she replied, and he did a double take at her flat stomach under the hospital gown. Where was she going to put all that food? "Oh, and if they have onion rings, I'll take a side of those, too. See, there's another vegetable I eat."

Apparently, her food preferences aligned more with a growing teenage boy than a consummate dieter. "Something to drink?"

"Strawberry milkshake, if they have it. If not, I'll just take a large orange soda. Oh, and a tapioca pudding. When I was ten, my dad had gallbladder surgery and I remember his hospital had the absolute best tapioca pudding in the world."

He tilted his head and wondered how she could remember a thing like the tapioca pudding she'd eaten when she was a kid, but not be able to remember that she'd never laid eyes on him before today.

When he didn't respond right away, her face turned a charming shade of pink and she pointed toward her purse. "Um, I have money in my wallet. I know it's kind of a big order and I'm not sure how we usually split costs—"

"I'm not taking your money," he interrupted loudly before she insulted him by implying that he'd let the woman he was marrying reimburse him for a meal. Not that he was actually marrying her. He ran a hand through his hair and lowered his voice. "I was just trying to figure out how to carry it all back to the room. Never mind. Don't worry about it. I'll hijack one of these tray tables or a wheelchair or something to push it on."

"Okay, then," she replied, not seeming to pick up on his sarcasm, or at least choosing to ignore it. "Can you hand me my cell phone before you leave? I should probably let my parents know what happened."

"Josselyn said she looked for your phone back at the office but only saw your purse."

"I don't suppose you have my parents' numbers in your contact list." She gnawed her lower lip, but Craig was saved from responding—as well as from staring at her sexy mouth—when she added, "Actually, they're probably out of cell range if my mom is still with the Khasi tribe. I'll just send them an email tomorrow."

"The Khasi tribe?"

"Yes. I'm sure she told you all about her latest research trip. Wait. You've met my parents, haven't you?"

"Uh, not in person. At least, not yet." There, that should be ambiguous enough. After all, Josselyn mentioned her folks were out of the country so it was plausible that he might've talked to them on the phone or via a video chat. Not that Craig knew the first thing about video chatting.

Caroline tilted her head at him. "What about you?"

"What about me?"

"I'm sure you probably need to call someone to let them know you're staying here overnight?"

He lifted a brow. "Like who?"

She shrugged, a deep V forming above her nose. "Do you live with anyone? Like roommates or your family or, um…me?"

His ribs squeezed with pity. It was bad enough that she couldn't remember the fact that they hadn't had sex. The poor thing really must be confused if she couldn't even recall whether they lived together.

It was on the tip of Craig's tongue to tell her that if they were sharing the same bed, he would've left a more lasting impression on her. Instead, he replied, "I live at my family's ranch in Thunder Canyon."

"Oh, good." She relaxed onto her pillows. "I was worried about who would take care of your cat while you're gone."

Craig took a couple steps forward and lowered his chin. "My cat?"

"Yeah, the one with only three legs!" Caroline exclaimed, her face brightening as though she'd just had a miraculous breakthrough in modern science. "I can't think of his name, but I'm sure it will come to me."

Disbelief and a slow-growing sense of alarm kept him from celebrating her achievement. How in the hell did this woman know about his pet? Not that it was completely inconceivable given the fact that most ranches had barns filled with various animals, but the three-legged part confounded him.

"Do you work there, too?" Caroline asked, seemingly ignoring the fact that Craig was staring at her with his mouth hanging open in shock.

"Where?" Craig gave his head a slight shake to clear his thoughts.

"At your family's ranch," she said slowly, as though it was *his* brain that had been concussed recently.

"Uh, yeah. We raise cattle."

Caroline got that satisfied, faraway look in her eyes again. Every time she made that face, Craig's collar seemed to shrink around his neck and his skin got all tight. Her next question made his toes twitch inside his boots. "So I really am going to marry a cowboy?"

Craig didn't know about that. She certainly wasn't going to marry *this* particular cowboy. No woman was. But he kept his jaw clenched as his feet fought the urge to run right past the sign for the cafeteria and straight toward the exit.

* * *

After several more tests, including an EEG before bed, Caroline was surprised by how soundly she slept through the night. Of course, anytime a nurse came to check on her or take her vital signs, all Caroline had to do was look over to where Craig was partially reclined in a too-small chair, his cowboy hat pulled low over his eyes. Then a bubble of security would surround her, making her happily drift back to sleep.

She felt rested when her first visitor arrived.

"Is our patient allowed to have chocolate croissants this morning?" Josselyn asked as she carried in a cardboard tray of coffee drinks in one hand and a white bag in the other.

"She most definitely is," Caroline said, sitting up straighter and resisting the urge to clap excitedly by adjusting the blanket across her lap.

Craig just grunted, before standing up to stretch. Judging by the frown on his face, he either wasn't a morning person or he didn't particularly care for flaky breakfast treats. Caroline hoped it was just the croissants because she couldn't imagine a cowboy not being an early riser. Actually, she couldn't imagine someone not liking fresh-baked pastries, either.

A cracking sound echoed through the room as he twisted at the waist. "I'm getting too old not to sleep in a bed anymore."

Caroline took a quick gulp of coffee to keep from asking the question on the tip of her tongue. How old was he? It was another thing she should know about her fiancé, but couldn't remember. He certainly didn't look old, but there were a few more creases around his eyes than most men her age might have.

"Thanks for bringing breakfast," Caroline said to Josselyn.

"I also brought you a pair of comfy pajamas and some toiletries, not knowing how long you'd be here." Josselyn patted the small tote bag resting against her hip. "Since I didn't have a key to your apartment, you'll have to make do with things from the superstore in Kalispell."

"Anything is better than this hospital gown," Caroline replied, suddenly curious about where her own clothes were. The ones she'd been wearing right before she'd hit her head. She was about to ask, but Dr. Robinson entered the room.

As the physician examined her, Caroline saw Craig slip into the hallway and pull out his cell phone. It was difficult following the doctor's penlight with her eyes when her gaze kept returning to Craig and the way his jeans cupped his rear end as he casually leaned against the nurses' station and spoke into his phone.

"So all the tests suggest that there isn't any long-term damage," Dr. Robinson said just as Craig returned to the room. "Any changes with your memory?"

As much as Caroline sensed the connection with Craig, there was also an underlying nagging sensation in the pit of her stomach every time she smiled at him and he looked away. Had they had a fight recently? Or maybe it was just the fact that she couldn't remember any clear details about the guy and she was projecting her own sense of guilt onto him.

"I feel like things are slowly starting to come back to me." Caroline was trying to remain positive but it was impossible not to notice the way Craig, Josselyn and the physician all looked at each other.

Dr. Robinson finally nodded. "Good. Everything should resolve itself eventually as long as you give your brain time to heal and don't add any additional stress."

The older woman gave a pointed look toward Craig, who scrubbed at the lower half of his face, where dark stubble had blossomed overnight.

"So then I can go home this morning?" Caroline couldn't keep the hopefulness from her voice.

"As long as you're not left alone. With the concussion, I want to be sure someone is keeping an eye on you."

"I have to be at the school library during the day." Josselyn spoke up. "But you can come stay with me out at Sunshine Farm until you're feeling more like your old self."

"I *do* feel like my old self," Caroline insisted, hating the sympathetic looks directed her way. "The only thing that's off is my memory about Craig, which means I should probably stay with him to help jog my brain."

Josselyn sucked in her cheeks before looking at Craig, whose eyes had gone dark again. However, the man kept his lips pressed firmly together. In fact, nobody said anything and it made Caroline wonder what was really going on. What weren't they all telling her?

Finally, Josselyn spoke up. "Craig, you're staying at your brother's ranch while you're in town, right?"

"Right," Craig agreed a little too quickly for someone who'd just been so hesitant to say a word. "I'm bunking with Will and his wife, Jordyn."

"That might be a little cramped, huh?" Josselyn nodded the answer at them as though she were talking to her kindergarten reading circle. "But there's plenty of room out at Sunshine Farm."

"There's also plenty of room at my own house," Caroline said as her gaze narrowed at them in suspicion. "Unless you guys aren't telling me why my fiancé shouldn't be staying with me there…"

Like perhaps Craig was planning to call off the engagement. Caroline's throat constricted.

Josselyn looked up to the ceiling, then said, "Well, here's the thing—"

"It's okay, Josselyn," Craig interrupted. "Of course I don't mind taking care of Caroline."

Chapter 5

Craig felt the heat of Josselyn's eyes on his back as they followed the discharge nurse who was pushing Caroline's wheelchair toward the parking lot. He knew his friend's wife-to-be was staring at him like he was nuts, but all he could do was shrug.

"What about your own ranch, Craig?" A muscle ticked in Josselyn's jaw as she kept her voice too low for Caroline to hear. "Shouldn't you be getting back to Thunder Canyon soon?"

"We just sold the bulk of our herd in Helena and breeding season won't start until after Christmas." Craig fished in his pocket for his truck keys. "My dad and Rob can handle things during the slow season. Besides, the doctor said this was only temporary. I'll be back home before next week."

"You know that you can't stay with Caroline at her place, right? She lives in the center of town and Rust Creek Falls is a small place. People will talk."

"I'll mention that to her when we get in the truck and head in that direction. I'm sure I can convince her during the drive that staying at my brother and sister-in-law's house is for the best."

Unfortunately, when they got to Will and Jordyn's ranch house, Craig realized his sweet and agreeable fiancée wasn't as easy to convince. And if he kept insisting, she was likely to counter his argument and then they'd both be stressed out.

Caroline stood in the middle of the small living room, one arm wrapped across her waist as she stared in confusion at her surroundings. "None of this looks familiar. Have I been here before?"

"Um, I don't think so." Craig regretted not putting a little more confidence into his voice.

He'd won the Professional Bull Riders World Championship two years in a row. When had he ever lacked confidence?

"Have I even met Will and Jordyn?" Caroline asked.

"I'm sure you have. Rust Creek Falls is a small town and chances are you've run into them before."

"You mean, you've never introduced us?" Caroline moved her hands to her hips and Craig suddenly wondered how he ever could've thought this petite woman was delicate or fragile. "Have you been keeping our engagement a secret from your family?"

When she turned her full glare at him, she looked eight inches taller than the five-foot-four height listed on her hospital admission paperwork. And a heck of a lot more intimidating than any bull he'd drawn during his time on the rodeo circuit. Craig knew this whole idea was crazy, and right now, he'd gladly welcome Josselyn's presence and her pointed looks of disbelief because that would at least take some of the attention off him. Or she'd at least help dig him out of this mess.

"It's not a secret. It just hasn't been that long since we became engaged." He flicked his eyes toward the clock on the wall. About twenty-four hours to be exact. Instead of keeping things closer to the truth, though, Craig added, "We were just waiting until the next family dinner to make our big announcement."

"And when exactly is the next family dinner?" One of Caroline's eyebrows shot up.

"Thanksgiving," he answered, then gave a silent prayer that Caroline would regain her memory by then.

Her lips parted as she blew out a puff of air, making her entire face soften. A shot of electricity zipped along his nerve endings. She really was a beautiful woman.

"Fine." She exhaled again. "I guess I can wait until next week to meet them all."

Wait. Next week? Damn, he hadn't realized how close the holiday was. That didn't give him much time to prove to Caroline that they really weren't engaged. Or for Caroline to regain her memory and figure it out for herself. For now, all Craig could do was offer a stiff smile and pray that he could untie himself from this lasso of deception that was twisting around him.

"Sorry for getting so snappy like that." She

lowered her arms and clasped her hands behind her back and he tried not to notice the way her dainty sweater looked much snugger on her when her proud shoulders were thrown back like that.

"No problem," he said because he couldn't very well just stand here letting her get worked up thinking they had an actual problem. Other than the problem that there was no possible way he was going to take some stranger to Thanksgiving dinner and have his entire family think they'd *both* lost their minds. Not that it was Caroline's fault she'd lost hers temporarily. But Craig didn't have the excuse of a concussion to explain his recent bout with irrational decisions.

"You have been so patient with me through all of this and don't deserve to have me doubting our entire relationship like this." She held out a palm when he opened his mouth to protest that he wasn't the saint she was making him out be. "I mean, obviously I'm experiencing this connection between us, but it's just so frustrating not being able to remember all the details of our life together."

Imagine how he felt. He was standing in his brother's living room with a woman he

didn't know, trying to keep her calm and relaxed as he pretended like he was her soon-
to-be husband.

Hold on. He pushed the brim of his hat
back on his forehead. "You're experiencing
a *connection*?"

"Of course I am. I didn't hit my head that
hard." Caroline rolled her eyes, then winced
as she brought her fingers to her temples.

Craig was by her side in an instant. "Does
it hurt?"

"Just when I move too quickly."

He put his hand on the small of her back
and tried to direct her toward the sofa. But
her pointy high heels didn't budge. Maybe a
strong wind wouldn't blow her over after all.
"Why don't you lie down and rest?"

"Actually, Craig, I would really feel more
comfortable if we just went back to my place."

"Honey, I can't very well stay the night at
your place with you. You know how people
love to gossip around small towns."

"Honey," she repeated before smiling wide.
She took a step toward him and his knees
went all rubbery, probably because he'd
hardly slept a wink in that hospital chair.
"That's what we call each other? I like it."

He rolled his lips inward to keep from admitting that it was the same term of endearment he used on all the young calves at the ranch when he was trying to herd them into a corral or lead them somewhere they didn't want to go. But she'd given him a lead and he didn't waste it. "Speaking of names people call each other, I would hate for anyone to say something unflattering about you if I were to spend the night at your house."

"Surely you know me well enough by now to realize that I don't care what people think about me." She waved a dismissive hand before resting her palm against his chest. A blast of heat lit underneath her fingertips and he stood there absolutely still, hoping the unfamiliar sensation passed. However, when she took another step closer to him and her eyelids lowered, the flame spread. "Plus, I'm sure it's not the first time we'll be staying the night together."

He gulped. "How do you figure?"

"How else would I know that you use two pillows?"

A jolt traveled down the back of Craig's neck as he wondered how she'd found out about his sleeping habits. Maybe that was just another good guess on her part. Plenty of people used more than one pillow.

"Anyway," she continued as her fingers made slow circles along the third button on his shirt, "I really think we would both be more comfortable at my place. Not to mention the fact that things are more likely to come back to me if I'm in my normal environment."

Craig searched her face, trying to control his breathing. The first problem was that if she continued touching him like this, there was no way he could remain in the same room with the woman, let alone the same house. At least, not unless he wanted to take their fake, temporary relationship to a real, permanent level. The second problem was that he had absolutely no idea where her house was, and he couldn't very well admit as much without further raising her suspicions.

While he may be willing to go along with this little delusion of hers to an extent, he wasn't about to have anyone believing that he didn't normally pick up his dates at their front doors like a gentleman.

When she was this close to him, it was impossible to concentrate on forming an acceptable excuse as to why he shouldn't stay with her. Only a weak-willed jerk would take advantage of a woman in this situation. And Craig had never been accused of being weak-willed.

"Please?" Her hands slipped up to his shoulders.

"Fine," Craig bit out, saying the only thing that would allow him to politely step out of her embrace and buy himself some more time. "Let me go get my gear and we'll head over to your place."

When he was in the spare bedroom packing up the duffel bag he'd brought to visit his brother, he shot off a text to Josselyn asking for Caroline's address. He shoved his toiletries in next, hoping that Joss wouldn't respond with a lecture on how he was making a massive mistake by taking Caroline home. Instead, the only thing she sent was an address to a smaller rental unit behind one of the historical houses in the heart of Rust Creek Falls.

"Ready to go?" he asked Caroline when he returned to the living room.

"Yes," she replied, setting down the picture frame she'd been studying. "Your family is huge."

He glanced at the photo of all his brothers

and sisters and their spouses at his parents' anniversary party last year. "There used to be just eight of us kids, but our numbers keep growing."

"And you're the oldest in the family?" she asked.

"Yep," he replied as he walked toward the front door, hoping she'd follow. Something prickled at him. Why would she automatically assume he was the oldest? Did he look elderly next to his siblings? Because he was beginning to feel that way when he was with her. According to the hospital bracelet still on her wrist, Caroline was only twenty-three, and suddenly he wondered if she was aware of the twelve-year age difference between them.

She picked up another frame, this time a picture of all his brothers at Jonathan and Dawn's wedding, then set it down before walking past him to get to the front porch. "Do you always look so solemn in your pictures?"

First she'd accused him of being proper, and now she was calling him solemn. Perhaps her "oldest in the family" comment was simply an accurate observation. After his rodeo career ended, everyone had begun referring to him as the stuffy, serious big brother.

"Well, someone has to be in charge and take care of the others. Besides, the photographer was taking forever to get the perfect grooms-men shot and all I wanted to do was get inside the reception and grab a beer."

"Speaking of photographers and recep-tions," Caroline said when Craig opened the truck door for her. "Have we started planning our wedding?"

He rubbed a hand on the side of his neck as he looked anywhere but at her face. Of course, she would've already been planning her wedding. It was what she did for a living. "I think you wanted to wait until after we told my family before we set a date."

"That makes sense." She nodded, and the ball of guilt that had slowly been building in Craig's gut got a little bigger.

He wanted to yell that none of it made any sense whatsoever. Instead, he climbed into the cab of his truck and steered toward Cedar Street, driving himself deeper into the next round of make-believe.

By the time he turned off Main Street, Craig had convinced himself that Caroline most likely had an actual fiancé or even a serious boyfriend who looked just like him. He was no brain surgeon, but it was truly the only way any of this could possibly make any sense. Josselyn had pointed out that Caroline wasn't wearing a ring, but that didn't mean anything nowadays.

When they got to her house, he was bound to see signs of whoever this mystery guy was. Of course, if there was in fact another man, Craig would need to figure out a way to explain why he'd gone along with the whole ruse.

He pulled into a long driveway of one of the large historical homes on Cedar Street and Caroline pointed toward the smaller cottage in the rear corner of the lot. "You can park in my space back here."

Her unit was a miniature version of the Craftsman-style house in front. There were well-tended flower bushes surrounding the green clapboard shingles, and a small cornucopia filled with mini pumpkins and colorful gourds sat on a table next to a white wooden rocking chair that was way too big for the dinky porch.

As Caroline unlocked the dark walnut door, Craig realized that this might be his last chance to make a run for it. There were no other vehicles parked near the property, but what if her real fiancé was sitting inside? Even a framed picture of another man with Caroline could be waiting in there, on full display to counter every falsehood he'd allowed the poor woman to believe about him.

Another unfamiliar pang of envy shot through him at the thought that this beautiful and optimistic woman might belong to someone else. Not that he should be jealous, he reminded himself as he cautiously followed her inside. If he didn't already know that Caroline was most definitely not his type, he would've been able to figure it out just by looking at her interior decorating choices.

There was an overstuffed white sofa in the middle of the living room and all Craig could think was how impractical the color was— it would be impossible to keep clean. Then there were the twenty or so throw pillows in varying floral and swirly prints piled on it, as well as the dollhouse-size chairs on either side of the full bookshelves that lined one entire wall. Okay, so maybe the chairs were a tad bigger than a doll, but he doubted they could hold all 190 pounds of him. Frilly yellow checkered curtains framed the windows, and expensive-looking paintings hung on the pale blue walls.

Craig had definitely been right about Caroline the first time he'd gotten a look at her silly high heels. A girlie girl like her would never last on the family ranch.

"I'm going to hop in the shower and wash the hospital smell off me," she said, setting her large tote bag down on the white kitchen table. "I think I have some deli meat in the fridge and I picked up a couple of bags of chips at the market a few days ago if you want to help yourself to a snack."

"I'm good," Craig said, trying not to think of what Caroline would look like naked, with the water sluicing off her.

Since the kitchen looked out into the living room, he guessed that the doorway she walked toward led to the bedroom. The only bedroom, judging by the look of things. That meant Craig would be bunking on the sofa tonight because there was no way he was going to sleep in a bed next to her, no matter how many pillows she thought she used.

He dropped his duffel bag near the sofa, and when he heard the water pipes hum to life, he began carefully examining the contents of the bookshelves. There were paperback novels shoved next to old-fashioned leather-bound volumes of those boring stories his high school English teacher referred to as "classics." There were ancient-looking artifacts and modern-looking sculptures. He recalled Josselyn mentioning something about Caroline's parents traveling quite a bit. She obviously had quite the collection of random souvenirs.

There were also plenty of framed photos of Caroline in all stages of her young life—from a pigtailed toddler to a college graduate—standing in between a proud man and woman who Craig assumed were her parents. He saw a handful of pictures of Caroline with other women her age, but there was nothing suggesting another man in her life.

His shoulders sagged in relief. Unfortunately, he didn't know if that relief was a good thing or a bad thing.

Chapter 6

Caroline wrapped her wet hair in a bun on top of her head and slipped on her favorite pair of cropped pink pajama pants. She debated putting on a bra, but her breasts were small enough that she could get away with a camisole-style tank. In the interest of modesty, she threw on her faded gray University of Montana sweatshirt, the one with the women's tennis team logo on the front.

While it was still the middle of the afternoon and she should want to impress Craig with her more fashionable wardrobe, she was pretty exhausted and just wanted to be comfortable. As a wedding planner, she always felt the need to be well put-together with a professional hairstyle and a businesslike appearance that conveyed to her clients that she could handle any situation. But she wasn't going into the office today.

Before she walked out of the only bathroom in her one-bedroom house, she swiped on a layer of mascara and applied some strawberry-flavored lip balm so she would at least look somewhat healthy.

She wasn't sure if her fiancé had seen her in her most natural state before, but if they were going to eventually be living together, he might as well get used to it. As she walked out of the bedroom, she found him staring at one of the oil paintings on her living room wall.

"My dad painted that when we lived in Nice," she said, going for her most casual voice since there was a chance she'd already told him the story about the café near the Sophia Antipolis. It was one thing to allow the guy to see her in comfy clothes; it was quite another to bore him to death with repeated anecdotes from her family's travels.

"You know what," Craig said suddenly,

taking a step back. "I'm going to go to the pharmacy and pick up your prescription."

"But I'm not having any pain right now. And I have some Tylenol in my medicine cabinet if I need it."

He couldn't seem to stop glancing toward the front door, and she wondered just how badly he was yearning to get away from her. Was it because of the plain way she looked? Or was something else going on with him? Not willing to be the source of his discomfort, she gave him an out. "Seriously, though, you really don't have to sit around here with me. I'm sure you have plenty of other things you could be doing on a Friday afternoon."

She couldn't tell if that was relief flashing across his face, but the short-lived expression was soon replaced with steely determination. "The doctor didn't want you to be left alone."

Caroline flicked her wrist. "But she didn't mean every single second. I'm sure you could leave and come back."

Despite the fact that *he'd* been the one who'd just suggested going to the pharmacy, he didn't appear convinced. So Caroline continued, "Actually, my phone and laptop are still at my office and if you could go and get those for me, I'd be able to get a little work done before tomorrow."

"What's tomorrow?"

"I'm meeting the organizers of the Presents for Patriots event. They're having a formal fund-raiser at Sawmill Station, and my company volunteered to host the event and coordinate the party planning."

Craig lowered his chin as he studied her. "I don't think you're supposed to be working yet."

"Well, my boss is out of town, so I'm the only one who can attend the meeting. Besides, most of the actual work is already done, but all the notes are on my laptop and I'd like to refresh myself with the details beforehand."

"Maybe I should call Josselyn and see if she can come over and watch you while I'm gone."

"Watch me? Like I need a babysitter?"

"Here we go again." Craig nodded at Caroline's arms, which were now crossed in front of her.

"What does that mean?" She narrowed her eyes at him. "Has my work schedule been a problem for you in the past?"

"In the past?" He mumbled something else under his breath but she didn't quite catch it.

"Or currently?" Her bare toes dug into the plush rug under her feet as she prepared to stay rooted to the spot until she got some answers.

"Um…" Craig took a step back.

"Please tell me you're not one of those old-fashioned macho types who think their women need to be taking care of the farm and raising their babies?"

"I don't even have a farm." Craig was now backed up against the arm of the sofa. "It's a ranch. And no, I don't have a problem with what you do for a living. You can work wherever and whenever you want. I was just concerned about your injury."

"Then what did you mean by 'here we go again'?"

"I meant that when you get determined to do something, you go from a sweet, docile little thing to some sort of broncing—I mean, fierce warrior like that." He snapped his fingers.

Broncing? Caroline really hoped that the man hadn't been about to compare her to an angry rodeo animal. They were both pretty worn-out, though, so she decided to give Craig the benefit of the doubt.

"Well, if it's any consolation, I rarely bring

out this so-called 'fierce warrior' unless absolutely necessary. At least not with most people." She tugged her lower lip between her teeth as she studied him. Then she asked, "Do we usually argue a lot?"

"What? No." One side of his mouth curled downward. "What would we have to argue about?"

"Sorry. Again." She felt her chest ease back, realizing she hadn't been aware she'd puffed it out in the first place. "I guess I'm just on edge because I'm pretty exhausted, even though it feels like I've been in a deep sleep for the majority of our engagement. Anyway, I was focusing on all the things I can't remember instead of being grateful for all the stuff that's clearly in front of me."

"In front of you?" Craig's skin seemed to lose some of its tan color.

"You." She rubbed his biceps in an effort to reassure him, but the physical contact only reminded her of how hard and well-shaped his muscles were under his shirt. She yanked her hand back a bit too quickly. "*You're* here in front of me. A wonderful man who was willing to spend the entire night in a miserable chair beside my hospital bed. A man who is willing to risk his proper reputation to spend the night with me at my house in order to nurse me back to health, even though I'm totally healthy, by the way."

He coughed. "Risking *my* reputation?"

Really, Craig was quite adorable when his eyebrow dipped into a squiggly line like that. Caroline had to wonder how often she confused the poor guy. Probably all the time if that was the cute face he made whenever she did.

"Thank you for being so good to me." She rose on her toes and kissed him on his cheek.

Craig didn't jump away from her in a desperate panic, but he also didn't return her kiss. He just stood there, stiff as a granite statue, his eyes dark and full of caution.

So far, she got the impression that he was definitely the type of guy who would be overprotective. She hoped his lack of response was because he didn't want to unleash his passion and accidentally injure her. The alternative would be that he didn't feel any passion for her at all, and Caroline didn't want to think about that dismal possibility.

"I'm going to go take a nap," she finally said, because one of them needed to say or do something. His only reaction was a brief nod.

As she walked to her bedroom, she was too nervous to turn around to look at him. But she listened to him unzip his duffel bag as her head hit the pillow. She fell asleep before she could hear anything else. When she woke up an hour later, she found a note by her bed.

Went to pick up your stuff from your office. Craig.

There was nothing about when he'd be back. Or if he'd even be back at all.

Craig was trying another key off the same ring Caroline had used to open her front door when his cell phone rang. Still standing in front of her office, he scrambled to pull the vibrating thing out of his back pocket, thinking Caroline had woken up and needed him. But she didn't have her cell phone, and he hadn't seen a landline at her house. In fact, she didn't even have his number. Which might present quite a problem once she realized the man she thought she was going to marry wasn't listed in any of her contacts.

Looking at the name on the display, Craig sighed before sliding his finger across the screen and answering. "Hey, Rob."

"Oh, good, you finally found time to answer your phone, big brother." Rob's voice always had a teasing edge, but today it was downright buoyant, as though nothing was going to sink his good humor. "Mom wants to know if you'll be bringing your new lady friend home for Thanksgiving."

Craig squeezed his eyes shut and counted to three. "What new lady friend?"

"The one our baby sister, Celeste, heard you had in the front seat of your truck about an hour or ago."

"How could C.C. hear about that already?" Craig asked, using the youngest Clifton's nickname. "She's not even home from college yet."

"Some kid from her vet science class used to babysit for Will's neighbor, who saw you with the pretty gal that works for that wedding planning outfit over at Sawmill Station. Said you both went into Will and Jordyn's house and then little bit later, you left together. With your duffel bag."

That was how things went in a small town. A neighbor told a friend, who told a cousin, who told their former fourth-grade teacher, and before a person could blink, it was on the front page of the *Rust Creek Falls Gazette*. He knew it was bound to happen. He just hadn't expected word to get all the way to Thunder Canyon that fast.

Stupid him.

"It's a long story, but there is absolutely nothing going on between me and Caroline Ruth." Craig immediately looked around the wooden platform in front of the old-fashioned train depot, hoping none of the Daltons, who owned the land, overheard the blatant lie. Clearly, there was *something* going on between him and the beautiful woman who, brain injury aside, should've known better than to kiss him. Even if it was only on his cheek.

Those sweet lips of hers held a promise of something more. What that was, Craig didn't want to know. Finding out wouldn't be fair to either of them, but especially not to Caroline, who looked incredibly innocent and fresh standing in front of him in those pajama pants that were so thin they showed the outline of her rear end. He didn't even want to start thinking about that sweatshirt that fell off her shoulder, displaying a slinky spaghetti strap against her smooth, creamy skin.

"Caroline Ruth," Rob repeated, his smug tone latching onto the slightest revelation of new information. "Good thing our grandfather is coming for dinner this year. He eats so slow, you'll have plenty of time to tell your family all about this so-called 'long story.'"

"Nothing to tell."

"Want to know what I think?" Rob asked.

"Actually, no. I don't really care what you th—"

"I think that there's *plenty* to tell about this Caroline Ruth and that's why you're trying to keep everything under wraps."

"Speaking of wraps, have those new posts come in yet for the southeast fence line?" Craig knew the best way to deal with his family was to redirect.

"Dad and I already took care of the fence," Rob replied, making Craig think that he'd successfully changed the subject. But his brother was like a mangy dog with a bone. "You know we're all going to find out about her anyway. Might as well come clean."

"Nothing much to tell." Craig scratched the scar tissue along his neck, thinking of ways to downplay the recent events that had completely bucked him like a greenhorn with his hand stuck in the bronc rein as he got dragged along for the ride. "Caroline is planning Drew and Josselyn's wedding. She took a pretty big fall in her office and smacked her head. When she came to, she thought she knew me, and the doctor said it was best not to correct her until she regained her memory."

"No way!" Rob whooped and Craig had to pull the phone away from his head before he ruptured an eardrum. "Like she's got amnesia? I didn't think that kind of thing happened in real life."

"It's not exactly amnesia," Craig started, before deciding it was probably best not to overexplain and get caught up in the details. "Anyway, that's why I said it was a long story. And I would appreciate it if you didn't tell anyone else what's going on. Caroline might not want strangers knowing her personal business."

"Right. So then how exactly did *you* get involved in her business?"

Craig sighed, but it came out as more of a growl. "Because her boss is out of town and her family's in another country and, with the concussion, the doctor didn't want her to be alone. So I gave her a ride home and I'm keeping an eye on things."

"Keeping an eye on things, huh?" Rob didn't bother to cover the mouthpiece on his end as he snorted.

"What's that supposed to mean?"

"You're my big brother. I know how you keep an eye on things. Growing up, you watched all of us like a hawk."

"I'm protective. So what?"

"*Protective* is an understatement, Craig. Remember the time we went to the county fair and Dad told you to watch us at the mutton busting competition? I was in third grade, but you told the judges I was only six because they made all the kids in that age bracket wear helmets."

"I'd like to point out that you were small for your age and the following year, they made everyone wear helmets. I was simply ahead of the times."

"Then," his brother continued, refusing to cede Craig's point, "you followed me into the pen and slipped the sheep I was riding a huge chunk of caramel apple. When the announcer blew the horn, instead of sprinting around the arena, the animal just stood there chewing its sticky cud."

"That sheep was nicknamed Wooly Widowmaker and I probably saved you from a broken arm and a lifetime of embarrassment. So, as much as I'd like to sit around and listen to you grovel out your eternal thanks, Rob, I actually need to get going."

"Anyway, back to the reason why I called. Are you bringing your new lady friend for Thanksgiving or not?" his brother asked.

"It depends."

"On what?"

Craig looked at Caroline's key ring hanging limply in the office door. "On whether she remembers who the hell I am before then."

Chapter 7

Caroline drenched the chicken pieces in flour as the oil sizzled in her cast-iron skillet. How could she remember the exact temperature for getting a perfect scorch on her fried chicken, yet not remember whether or not her fiancé even liked her cooking?

Glancing at the digital clock on the stove, Caroline realized that she was stressing about what to feed Craig when she should be worried about the fact that he might not be coming back at all.

No. Of course he would come back. Her gut knew it, even if her head was slow to see all the other signs. He'd sat with her in the hospital all night. If he was going to bail out on her, he would've done it long before now.

She'd spent the past hour walking around her house, looking in drawers and pulling out old family photo albums, gaining more comfort and confidence each time she'd come across another detail in her life that she recalled clear as day. If she had her laptop, she would get online and do some research on amnesia and concussions and anything else that could be wrong with her brain.

Not that anything else seemed to be wrong. As far as she could tell, Craig was the only person in her world that she didn't remember. Sure, it was disconcerting, but it would've been downright eerie if she didn't have that steady sensation that there was definitely something about the man that felt right.

Turning up the volume on the music channel on her television, Caroline sang along with the classic country station, taking further solace in the fact that she still knew all the words to every George Jones, Dolly Parton and Conway Twitty song by heart.

When Tammy Wynette came on and encouraged her to stand by her man, Caroline hiccuped a little giggle. Her mother had once caught her only child listening to that particular song and immediately put on her Helen Reddy CD and had her daughter memorize the lyrics to "I Am Woman" instead.

Caroline really needed to email her parents. She'd video chatted with them on Monday, but they never went more than four or five days without at least a text conversation. They were bound to get worried if they didn't hear from her soon. Not that Caroline would tell them about being in the hospital. Her dad had a writer's imagination and she didn't need him thinking the worst and flying back to the States early just to check on her.

A light knock sounded at the door and she padded out of the kitchen in her pink fuzzy slippers. Looking through the peephole, she felt a charge of excitement surge through her when she saw Craig standing on her porch.

"You didn't have to knock," she told him as she yanked the door open so quickly, it bumped against her shoulder. "I left it unlocked for you."

"I didn't want to just barge in and scare you, especially if you were still asleep."

"I'm awake." She smiled, then felt her lips

falter as she realized she was standing there like an eager cocker spaniel, stating the obvious. Caroline stepped aside to let him into the house.

Craig handed her the laptop case and her smartphone with twenty-four missed calls and twice as many text alerts. He sniffed and asked, "Are you cooking something?"

Caroline was still leaning against the open door frame and the chilly air reminded her that she'd taken off her sweatshirt when she'd started working in the kitchen. Craig's eyes dropped to where her hardened nipples pressed against the soft cotton fabric of her tank top. However, instead of shivering from the cold, Caroline was filled with a rush of warmth from his intense stare.

If it had been any other person standing there, she would've clutched the laptop to her chest and blocked his view. But there was something slightly empowering about having this type of effect on her man. Overcome with a boldness she couldn't explain, Caroline pushed her shoulders back, making her small breasts thrust further out. She saw the muscles in his throat swallow and then she actually did shiver.

"Yes," she finally said, then spoke louder.

"I'm making fried chicken and mashed potatoes. I wasn't sure what you liked to eat so I hope that's okay?"

Walking toward the kitchen, she set her laptop down on the dining table along the way. She heard Craig closing the front door and wondered if she should've also grabbed her sweatshirt off the back of the sofa and covered up. Even though they were engaged, she was completely alone in her house with the man. A man who looked at her as though she was the most attractive woman in the world and he was just now seeing her for the first time.

Of course that was silly on both accounts— she was by no means beautiful and, obviously, Craig had seen her before. But why did it suddenly feel as though she was now playing with fire?

Trying to ignore all these unfamiliar emotions battling inside her, Caroline flipped the chicken over in her trusty skillet, needing to ground herself in something she understood. Food.

A tingling crept up the back of her neck and she glanced over her shoulder, spotting Craig leaning one of his jean-clad hips against the counter.

"That's my favorite," he said, still staring at her, his nostrils slightly flared.

Caroline's mouth went dry. "What is?"

"Fried chicken." But his dark blue eyes weren't focused on the food in the pan. They were studying her and all that lovely heat was spreading through her body again. "You asked if it was okay."

"Oh." Caroline forced her own attention back to the stove.

"Do you need any help in here?" he asked.

She allowed her head to turn only slightly in his direction. "You know how to cook?"

"Of course. I'm the oldest of eight kids and I grew up on a ranch. My parents made all of us learn how to do every job around the place from wrestling steers to feeding baby calves to churning homemade butter."

"When I was a kid, I didn't even have baby dolls to take care of. I wish I had grown up with siblings. What was that like?"

"Trust me, my brothers and sisters were way more needy and annoying than baby dolls. But once in a while, they would come in handy when we had a lot of chores to do."

"Are ranches a lot of work?" she asked, wanting to keep the conversation off anything that would make her think about how close he was to her in this tiny kitchen.

"You have no idea." Craig made a weird huffy sound that came out as a chuckle. It was the same noise her college roommate had made when Caroline enrolled in the same linear algebra class as the serious math major. By the end of the semester, the roommate was coming to Caroline for tutoring.

There were few things in this world that Caroline actually found to be all that challenging once she set her mind to it. So when someone implied that she couldn't handle something, it only made her want to master that very thing. It didn't matter if it was ranching, advanced mathematics or mashing some potatoes while a sexy cowboy stood so close, her tummy felt like it was doing flips.

Oh, and she could also do flips, thanks to her years on two different junior high gymnastics teams.

She was tempted to say as much to Craig, but it was always easier to just show people what she could do. Although she had to admit that she'd been the first one to question *his* abilities when he'd offered to help her cook.

Instead, Caroline forced a smile and told

her fiancé, "I've got things under control in here."

"Oh. Okay." He put his hands in his back pockets and she turned to the fridge to pull out more ingredients for the potatoes. She was reaching for a pint of half-and-half when he added, "Then would you mind if I used your shower?"

She turned around so quickly, the carton of butter she'd been holding slipped out of her grip, and one of the sticks popped out and landed near the toe of his cowboy boot. Before he could bend down to pick it up, she was already forming an image of a very naked Craig in her small, steamy bathroom.

"Unless you'd rather I stay here to help," he said, holding out the butter that was still wrapped in its wax paper, one corner completely dented. It was then that she noticed he was wearing the same clothes he'd had on at the hospital yesterday. No wonder he wanted to take them off. She stared at the buttons on his shirt, thinking how easy it would be to slip them through their little holes and... *Stop*, she commanded herself, then drew in a deep gulp of air and found her voice.

"No, I'm fine. I'll get you a towel as soon

as I turn the heat down in here," she offered, then caught her breath at the double meaning. "The heat on the stove, I mean. Unless you already know where the towels are. Assuming you've taken a shower here before. Not that you would have, unless there was a time when you needed to. Although how would I know either way? It's not like I've been giving a lot of thought to you being in my shower. And now I'm just babbling and not making sense at all. I better just show you where the linen cabinet is."

Except he didn't seem the least bit confused by her rambling, awkward speech. In fact, his normally questioning eyebrow remained firmly in place as he lifted one side of his mouth and replied, "I think I can figure it out."

Caroline Ruth had almost as many bottles lined up on her tiled shower wall as she did on the narrow shelf above her pedestal sink. Although he'd never shared a bathroom with his sisters, Craig knew perfectly well that women tended to like a variety of beauty products, especially ones that smelled good. However, the amount of choices on display before him had to be some sort of record.

Craig sniffed at the open lid of the fancy shampoo. At least, he assumed it was fancy judging by the French label. He also assumed it was shampoo since he didn't speak French. But it wasn't like he was some young, inexperienced buck. He was thirty-five years old and had stayed the night at ladies' places before. But that was mostly when he'd been traveling on the pro circuit, and he usually did so only after a night out celebrating a good ride. Then he'd be back on the road, heading for the next city. He'd never really been all that invested in a relationship enough to pay much attention to what the women he dated stocked in their bathrooms.

Well, except for Tina. She'd been his neighbor and they'd practically grown up at each other's houses. Tina had been the type to use whatever soap was on sale at the local market. It was why she'd been the perfect partner for Craig. She didn't care about all these frilly, girlie things like—he squinted his eyes at the label across the white bottle he'd just knocked over—Paraben-Free Volumizing Conditioner with Added Boost. She cared about horses and working hard and merging her family's ranch with his. Unfortunately,

Craig's dream of the perfect partnership and the perfect relationship had died along with Tina many years ago.

Pretending otherwise with Caroline wasn't fair to either of them.

Foregoing the shampoo bottle's posted recommendation of a five-minute wait time, Craig stuck his head under the nozzle to rinse off. Then he turned the water as hot as he could stand it, hoping the steam would drive away all the cravings the pretty wedding planner had recently brought back into his world.

His skin was red and stinging when he finally shut off the water. Maybe he should've taken a cold shower instead. He grabbed a fluffy lavender towel—because apparently there was nothing masculine in this house—and wrapped it around his waist. Wiping his hand across the fogged-up mirror above the sink, Craig stared at his reflection.

What was he doing here?

He needed to go out there and tell Caroline the truth. He needed to call Josselyn or Drew or Dr. Robinson and inform them that he couldn't do this. He couldn't keep lying to that poor, sweet girl.

No. She wasn't a girl, he reminded himself as he saw an edge of lace peeking out from behind the damp towel hanging off a hook on the back of the door. She was a woman. A woman who clearly wasn't wearing a bra right this second. And he'd boldly stared at her small, firm breasts as though he'd had a right to look. He'd stood there in her open doorway wondering what shade of pink her nipples would be as his palms had itched to slide up underneath her skimpy tank top.

Now that his body recalled the image, he had to refasten his towel over his growing arousal. Cursing, he dug into his duffel bag to pull out his shaving kit and ended up knocking the whole thing off the toilet. This bathroom was so tiny.

Hell, the whole house was tiny. It felt as if everything was shrinking in on him. How was he going to last the entire night with Caroline and not accidentally touch her? There had to be someone else who could stay here with her.

As though reading his exact thoughts, Craig's phone lit up with an incoming text from Drew. How's our patient?

She seems to be completely fine, Craig's

big fingers tapped out awkwardly on the mi-
nuscule keyboard.

It was the truth. Caroline looked totally
healthy. Almost too healthy, if one asked
Craig's growing libido. He stared at his
screen, hoping that his buddy would give him
permission to abandon his caregiver duties.

Head injuries are like that. They can seem
fine one minute, and the next minute... Drew
didn't finish his sentence, letting three little
dots at the end of his sentence imply all the
potential risks to Caroline.

Those three dots were the reason Craig was
here. Nobody knew what to expect.

When Craig didn't reply, another text bubble appeared from Drew. Has she regained
her memory yet?

As far as I can tell, she knows everything else
about her past except who I am. It's weird.

The brain is a weird and complex thing.

Thanks for the anatomy lesson, Dr. Drew. But
what do I do in the meantime? I can't keep pretending that we're engaged.

What else do you have going on right now?

Craig pushed a lock of wet hair off his forehead before typing, It's not a matter of my time.

You want me to see if Ben can come stay with her?

Even with all the hot air surrounding him, Craig went cold at the thought. No, he typed and hit the send button.

It's me she wants, not Ben, he began typing, then immediately deleted the words. That would make him sound jealous when he clearly had nothing to be jealous of because none of this was real. Caroline didn't truly want him. She didn't even know him.

It's that none of this feels right. She's going to be so pissed when she finds out we have been tricking her, Craig wrote instead, purposely using the word *we* to remind Drew that he was in on this asinine plan.

There was no response for a while, so Craig set his phone down and lathered his face. He was halfway done shaving when Drew's next text came through. Just try to be as honest as possible without stressing her out. And remember, it's not YOU tricking her. It's her brain.

But why did her brain pick me? he replied. Not that he would've preferred it picking Ben.

This time, he didn't have to wait long for Drew's response. Buddy, I may be a doctor, but even someone as smart as me doesn't know why ANY woman's brain would pick you.

Haha, Craig texted, then added an emoji of a hand making a crude gesture. That was pretty much the extent of his technology skills.

He finished shaving and found a clean pair of jeans in his duffel bag. However, all the steam in the enclosed space made his skin damp and he had to wrestle the jeans over his legs. After he finally buttoned his fly, he decided he needed to let in some cool air before pulling on one of his T-shirts.

When he opened the bathroom door, Caroline stood on the other side, one arm raised as though she'd been about to knock. At first, her eyes were round with surprise, but then her lids lowered toward his bare chest. He resisted the urge to flex his pectoral muscles, but he also couldn't bring himself to break her concentration as she studied him, a slight hitch in her breathing. After all, it had been a while since his body was whole. Since a woman had been so obviously and physically responsive in her assessment of him.

They stared at each other for what felt like minutes before she finally squeaked, "Dinner's ready."

Caroline pivoted quickly and her slim legs practically ran toward the living room. When she was finally a safe distance away, Craig's only thought was that if they both kept looking at each other like that, they would never get through the night.

Chapter 8

After accidentally confirming that every ounce of his upper torso was indeed made out of rippling muscle, Caroline decided that she couldn't face Craig across the dining table and carry on a conversation without thinking of his steamy tan skin underneath his T-shirt.

"Why don't we put something on TV while we eat?" she suggested, carrying their plates to the coffee table she'd found at a local antiques store and painted a soft shade of butter yellow.

"Wow, this looks great," he said when he sat next to her on the sofa, which was really more of a love seat. It was too late when she realized that being this close to him, sitting side by side, was almost as bad as making eye contact with him.

"What do you want to watch?" she asked when he had a forkful of mashed potatoes and gravy in his mouth, then had to wait for him to finish chewing before he could answer.

"I don't care. What do you normally watch?"

"Whatever I programmed on the DVR the week before." She picked up the remote control and turned on the television and a list of her new recordings popped up on the screen.

He let out a little chuckle. "Looks like my choices are either all of last Saturday's college football games or else an assortment of movies from the Hallmark Channel."

"That'd be pretty much it," she said, scrolling down. "I'm guessing you don't want to watch this one about a big shot fashion designer returning to the small town where she grew up to attend her former prom date's wedding to another woman?"

"Pretty sure I already read the book," Craig said before biting into a crispy chicken thigh. His thick lashes actually fluttered closed as he moaned.

"So football, then?" Caroline said brightly, turning up the volume so the sportscasters drowned out Craig's sighs of satisfaction.

"Sure," Craig said as he wiped his hands on a napkin. "But I already watched the University of Montana game last Saturday."

"I know they lost, but they're still the top seed in the Big Sky Conference, and if they beat Portland State next week, they'll go to the FCS playoffs."

"Wait. You actually watch college football?" The squiggly eyebrow was back, but instead of looking surprised, his accompanying smirk made him appear doubtful.

"Craig, my parents have been guest lecturers at most of the top universities in the United States. So I've been to a football game at every Division 1 stadium and most of the Division 2 schools."

"Wow. I guess I didn't see that coming."

"Seems as if we're both still learning things about each other." She smiled as she picked up a piece of chicken.

"Why don't we see what's on live TV?" he suggested and then shoveled another forkful of potatoes into his mouth. "This gravy is almost as good as my grandma's."

"Almost?"

"Well, it's better, but don't tell my Meemaw."

"Will I be meeting your Meemaw at Thanksgiving?" Caroline tried to get her voice as neutral as possible. Now that the subject of his family had come up again, she didn't want to seem too eager or even pushy. But she was dying to know more about the rest of the Cliftons. It would give her more clues about the man she was planning to marry.

"Probably. Unless she and my grandpa get into one of their fights beforehand. Even then, she might still show up just to make him mad. If they *are* going at it, though, you have to be very careful not to pick sides."

"Please. I'm a wedding planner. Diplomacy during the heat of family disputes is my specialty." She pushed the live-TV button on the remote control and since it was already set to a sports channel, an announcer welcomed them to the North American Championship Rodeo. "How long have your grandparents been married?"

"Oh, they aren't married to each other. Meemaw is my grandma on my mom's side and Grandpac is my dad's dad."

"His name is Grand Pack? Two words?"

"No." Craig gave a slight grin and Caroline realized it was the first time she'd seen him not looking so blasted serious. Her knees would've gone all wobbly if she hadn't already been sitting down. "Grandpac. One word. When I was a kid in Wrangler Camp, we had to learn how to work with leather, and I decided to hand tool Grandpa Clifton's name onto the back of a belt. Unfortunately, as I started running out of room, my letters got squished closer together and I could only fit *Grandpa C*, which ended up looking more like *Grandpac*. My brother Jonathan had just learned to read, and when he sounded it out as one word, the name just kinda stuck."

"Aw." Caroline's rib cage felt all warm and liquidy, just like her gravy. "I bet your Grandpac was so proud to wear something you made especially for him."

"Oh, no, he couldn't actually wear it. My grandfather is a man of considerable stature." Craig extended his arms into a circle in front of his belly for emphasis. "And I'd used myself as the model and then added two inches because I had absolutely no concept of waist sizing. But he did put it in a display case and still brings it out every time Meemaw wears the feather-and-bead earrings I made her."

"That's sweet that your grandparents love showing off the gifts you made them."

He shook his head, but kept glancing at the television as he spoke. "It's not sweet, it's calculated. They've never gotten along and are always competing with each other to be the favorite grandparent. It usually means lots of great presents at Christmas and birthdays, but the rest of the year we all just try to get out of the room as soon as the bickering starts."

Craig shrugged before directing all of his attention at the bull rider on the screen and effectively ending any further discussion.

She finished eating and soon lost interest in whatever the commentator with the turquoise bolo tie was saying about the combined score in the short go-round. Plus, Caroline still needed to email her parents and look over her notes for tomorrow's meeting at work. Craig didn't seem to notice as she stood up and retrieved her laptop off the dining room table. When she settled back onto the couch, she powered on the computer and got to work.

At some point she'd brought her legs up into a crisscross position and Craig's elbow ended up resting on her knee. Caroline enjoyed the discovery that they could spend a pleasant, ordinary evening side by side, in companionable silence. At least, they were enjoying it until the announcer said, "Our next rider is on pace to beat the record for consecutive rides, a record that was set six years ago by Craig Clifton before he retired from the pro circuit."

At the mention of her fiancé's name, Caroline lifted her head in time to see an image of a younger Craig flash on the screen.

"That's you!" she said, pointing to the TV.

"Yep." His hand slipped between their bodies and Caroline held her breath, wondering if he was finally going to make some sort of move. Instead, he found the remote wedged into the cushions and hit the power button. "It's getting pretty late, huh?"

"I didn't know you rode in the rodeo," she said, pivoting her upper body toward him and resting an arm across the back of the sofa.

He wasn't rude enough to point out the obvious—that there were actually a lot of things she didn't know about him. But he also didn't seem particularly inclined to provide her with the details, either.

"Is that how you got your scar?" She had barely traced the hook shape when he pulled away.

"I'm going to do the dishes," he said, his hip knocking into her knee as he stood up quickly. Carrying their plates into the kitchen, he glanced back at her with a pointed look and added, "You should probably get to bed."

The guy had barely said two words for the past hour and now he only spoke when he wanted to boss her around. Caroline stood up and followed him, remaining on the opposite side of the kitchen counter that separated the sink from the rest of the living area. "What about you?"

"What about me?" he asked, not bothering to look up as he rinsed off their silverware.

"Are you coming to bed?"

"I'll go to sleep after I clean up the kitchen." Craig was proving to have quite the habit of carefully phrasing his answers.

Caroline angled her head, trying not to let the frustration settle onto her expression. "But where will you be sleeping?"

"I can bunk on the couch." He might have shrugged, but it was too difficult to tell since he was leaning sideways to load the dishwasher.

"It's more of a love seat," she replied, estimating that he had to be at least six feet tall. "I mean, it can fold out into a bed but the mattress is thin and the frame is kind of wonky with the support bar going right across the middle."

"I've slept on worse," he replied, his knuckles turning white as he tightly gripped the cast-iron skillet.

"Yeah, but don't you think you'd be more comfortable in my bed?" The words were out of her mouth before she could stop them. It wasn't exactly like she was eager to hop into bed with the man she was still trying to remember. But she also recalled his comment this morning about his back and she didn't want him spending another night in agony.

Besides, she was learning that she never got any answers out of Craig unless she pushed him.

"Here's the thing, Caroline." Craig glanced toward the bedroom, but when he faced her, he wouldn't meet her eyes. A pit settled into her stomach as she realized the answer before he said it. "We haven't slept together yet."

Craig hated the fact that he'd obviously brought that shocking pink color to her cheeks last night, but there had been absolutely no way he could've lain next to her in a bed all night and maintained his distance.

Hell, he was having a hard time maintaining his distance this morning as the scent of sizzling bacon woke him from his crooked sleep on the uncomfortable sofa bed. Caroline stood in front of the stove, stirring scrambled eggs in her cast-iron skillet, looking like one of those old-fashioned housewives from the *Leave It to Beaver* era.

A silky, flowery dress hugged her backside before flaring out above her knees, and she had another pair of high heels on her feet. Who dressed like that to cook breakfast?

When she turned around to pass him a mug of hot coffee, he noticed that a white apron with a cherry print covered the front of her dress. Her brown hair was clipped away from her face and fell in soft waves down her back. Craig didn't know what looked more appealing—her or the plate of perfectly crisped bacon she handed him next.

If he hadn't already seen how much food she could put away in her petite frame, he would've assumed that she was trying to impress him with her cooking skills. But since she divided the eggs into equal portions on their plates, it was obvious that she enjoyed food as much as he did.

"What time do you need to be at your office this morning?" he asked.

"I was hoping to go in around eight and get things set up for the meeting."

He glanced at the digital clock on the stove. "That was thirty minutes ago."

"I know, but I don't have my car and you were out cold on the sofa bed, so I didn't have the heart to wake you."

Craig rubbed his neck and tried not to think of the stiffness in his back that had kept him awake the first half of the night. Well, it was his aching muscles along with a side of guilt and a constant awareness of Caroline's physical proximity that had kept him from getting to sleep before two in the morning.

"Let me just grab a quick shower and I'll take you," he offered before carrying his coffee into the bathroom with him.

Fifteen minutes later, he was backing his truck out of the long driveway and she was handing him an English muffin filled with the eggs and bacon he hadn't wanted to take the time to eat.

When he pulled into the gravel parking

lot at Sawmill Station, her little blue MINI Cooper was the only vehicle there. Just as it had been yesterday afternoon. Grabbing her laptop case out of his crew cab, Craig followed her inside the former one-room train depot that served as her office. The Daltons had bought the surrounding land last year for their ranching operation, but because the train depot and the larger freight house next door were historical landmarks, they couldn't tear them down. From what Craig understood, Vivienne, Cole Dalton's wife, had moved her wedding planning business to Rust Creek Falls and they now used the space to hold big parties.

Perfectly good waste of grazing land, if you asked Craig.

"You don't need to hang around," she said, flipping on the lights and setting a bright yellow tote bag—similar to the one she'd had yesterday—on an antique desk with fancy scrollwork.

"But there's no one else here," he said, dropping to his knees beside a modern woodburning stove in the corner. It was freezing in this place.

"I know, but Brendan and Fiona will be

here soon. Plus, it's not like I'm at risk of falling asleep or knocking myself out. Again."

"But the doctor said we shouldn't leave you alone," he reminded her.

"Did she say for how long?"

"Not exactly. Though I was under the impression that you needed someone with you until you got your memory back."

"But, Craig," she said as she smiled, "I *do* have my memory back. Or at least most of it."

So then why did she still think they were engaged? He wanted to ask her as much, but he didn't know how to without it sounding like some sort of test. Plus, he heard a car pull into the lot outside.

He got the fire going and rose up just as Brendan Tanner and his girlfriend, Fiona O'Reilly, walked inside. They greeted Caroline first, and when Fiona turned Craig's way, she did a double take.

"Hey there, Craig. I wasn't expecting to see you here." Fiona's family owned a local ranch, and when Craig had been stuck in the hospital with Caroline and bored out of his mind, he'd read one of her online articles about the free-range grazing habits of Herefords. "Are you volunteering for the Presents for Patriots fund-raiser, too?"

"Nope," Craig answered a bit too quickly and his single syllable response did nothing to wipe the curious expression from Fiona's face.

"My car got left here in the parking lot, so Craig had to give me a ride to work this morning." Caroline's explanation wasn't helping the matter, either. He held his breath as his supposed fiancée turned toward him. "You're more than welcome to stay, honey, but I'm sure you have other things you need to do today."

There was a slight gasp at her use of the endearment and he realized that it had come from his own mouth.

That settled it. There was no way Craig was sticking around and waiting for Brendan and Fiona's questions that would be sure to follow. He squared his shoulders and took Caroline up on her suggestion that he leave.

"Okay, then I'm going to head over to the Daltons' stable and talk to them about their new longhorn." It was his way of letting her know that he'd still be nearby if she needed him.

"We're supposed to be meeting Bailey Stockton here," Brendan called out to Craig, who paused as he made his way toward the exit. "So if you see a guy in the parking lot who looks like he's got a chip on his shoulder and would prefer to be out riding horses instead of inside talking to actual humans, go ahead and point him in this direction."

Craig knew some of the Stocktons from his past visits to Rust Creek Falls, but not Bailey. He was the most recent one to move to town, and Craig didn't blame the guy for wanting to get as far away from the wedding planner's office as possible. In fact, if Craig *did* run across the man, he'd probably invite him to hop in the truck with him so they could both get the hell out of Dodge.

Chapter 9

No sooner had Caroline heard Brendan and Fiona pull away in their car than Craig swung the office door wide-open, bringing in the crisp late-afternoon autumn breeze. In fact, if she didn't know any better, she'd think he'd been purposely waiting for the others to leave before rushing back to her rescue.

It was on the tip of her tongue to remind him that she was more than capable of being by herself for a few minutes, but when she saw him standing before her in his dusty jeans and sweat-soaked T-shirt, her heart sent a little flutter along her nerves.

"Why are you all dirty?"

"The Daltons got a young bull this morning and he was pretty testy about there being a buffer field between the steer pasture and the heifers in the grazing pasture. Young buck busted through the first fence and was scratching his head against the second when I got there, totally oblivious to the thousands of jolts zapping him. I had to help get him back in the pen while they retrenched the ground posts and ran the galvanized wires deeper underground to conduct a stronger current."

"I literally have no idea what you just said," Caroline said.

"Basically, one of their new bulls got loose and was trying to get to the female herd to get a jump start on the breeding season. We had to calm him down and then fix the electric fencing so that he wouldn't try it again."

"And here, I didn't need an electric fence at all," Caroline mumbled under her breath. Last night, Craig had made it clear that he didn't require any sort of buffer zone to stay well clear of her bedroom.

"What was that?" he asked, stepping inside and closing the door behind him.

She couldn't very well admit that she'd actually been comparing him to an overexcited farm animal. Or feeling jealous of whichever lucky cow had been on the receiving end of that bull's pent-up desire. "I just need to power off my computer and grab a couple of files and then I'll be ready to go," she said instead.

"No problem," he said. His boots paced over the wood floorboards as he walked toward the bookshelf. "I hope you didn't stand on any chairs today."

"Nope. Everything was on the lower shelves."

"Did you eat lunch?" he asked.

"Actually, we had a menu tasting with the caterer who is doing the fund-raiser. I saved you a portion of beef Wellington, but when you didn't come back by two o'clock, I assumed you were eating with the Daltons. Plus, Bailey Stockton was getting pretty antsy, so I gave him your food. But if you're hungry, we can stop at Buffalo Bart's on the way home and get some wings. Or if you're sick of chicken, I can whip up a lasagna for dinner."

"You say 'whip up a lasagna' like it's the easiest thing in the world to make."

Caroline shrugged as she took a step closer

to him, wondering if he normally kissed her hello at the end of a workday. "I like cooking. It gives my hands something to focus on so that my brain can work on all the bigger things."

"Speaking of your brain, how's your head been feeling today?" He reached out to trace a finger across her forehead and she all but sighed and leaned into his hand. "Any headaches?"

"Nope," she replied, using his favorite word. She must've fallen in love with his protective and caring nature, because she certainly hadn't fallen in love with his quiet and aloof conversation style. Actually, he was not always reserved when he was speaking. If the topic involved ranches and cattle, he could go on for days.

But when he touched her tenderly like this, or studied her with those blue eyes dark with concern, he didn't need to use any sort of conversation. Her thighs trembled and she felt as if she could actually pass out. Again.

"You okay?" he asked, cupping her elbow. "I should've known putting in a full day at the office would be too much for you."

No, it was being too close to him—breathing in his musky fragrance of hard work and the outdoors—that was making Caroline suddenly grow weak. "Craig, I promise I'm perfectly healthy."

He took a step back, yet watched her carefully as she gathered her things—as though he wasn't the least bit convinced that she wasn't going to collapse at his feet at any minute.

Then, later that evening, when they were again sitting side by side watching television while they ate dinner, Craig kept his body practically glued to the opposite end of the sofa. It was almost as though he was worried that if he touched her, she would completely go to pieces.

Steeling her spine, she turned toward him to tell him as much. "I've been noticing that you've been keeping your distance from me lately."

"Lately?" he asked, but his tone wasn't incredulous as much as it was sarcastic, suggesting that the word was some sort of understatement.

"Ever since my accident, you back up every time I move closer to you," she said, then scooted across the cushion to prove her point. Since the armrest prevented him from moving any more to the left, he shot forward, knocking his knee into the coffee table. "See? Every time. That's exactly what you do."

"What am I doing?" he asked, standing up with their plates.

"You're trying to get as far away from me as you can."

He opened his mouth as though to deny it, but nothing came out. She also stood and took the plates from him and set them back onto the table. Then she swallowed the last bit of orange soda in her glass, wishing it was merlot for an extra boost of courage, before turning back to him and placing her palms on the fresh shirt he'd put on after his shower.

"You know, Craig, I won't break if you kiss me."

Craig had to fight every impulse and muscle in his legs to keep from stepping back and well out of kissing range. Not that Caroline was actively trying to plant her lips on his, but she was blinking those intoxicating eyes at him and pouting her pretty little mouth, the invitation clearly extended.

"I just think that maybe we should wait for…" For what? Why would an engaged couple wait to kiss each other? The problem was that they weren't the average engaged couple. Or even a couple at all. He seized on that logic. "I was just waiting until you regained your memory. I don't want it to feel like you're kissing a stranger."

As impossible as it was, the small living room got even smaller, and it felt as though a cinch belt was squeezing across Craig's chest, tethering him in place. There was no way Caroline was buying any of this.

"I know I don't remember you, but how could I ever think of you as a stranger? Even if I'd never laid eyes on you before I'd hit my head," she continued and he froze, wondering if she was aware of how close she was to the truth. But instead of going with that more accurate description of the relationship, she slid her palms up to his shoulders and countered, "We've spent the past forty-eight hours together."

He looked at the digital readout on the cable box. "More like sixty hours."

"My point is that a loving heart is the truest wisdom."

Huh? Were they talking about hearts or wisdom here? Because in Craig's mind, the two never seemed to work well together. "I'm not following you."

"It's a quote by Charles Dickens. He's my dad's favorite author and I was named after one of his books."

"Still doesn't make any of this clearer," Craig replied.

"What I'm trying to say is that your actions these past two days speak louder than anything else, and my heart already knows everything it needs to know about you based on how well you've cared for me." Her thumbs traced circles above his shoulder blades and she asked, "Why are your muscles so tight?"

"Because I'm trying really hard not to move right now." There was absolutely nothing stopping him from walking straight out her door, yet he'd never felt more trapped.

As much as he'd fought it, his attraction to Caroline was like that headstrong young bull trying to bust out of its corral today. Obviously, Craig didn't believe in any of that nonsense about her having a wise heart or his actions speaking loudly or whatever else it was she was suggesting. But there was some sort of unexplainable connection between them. Some sort of magical fencing that zapped at his senses if he so much as moved, so much as acted upon this attraction.

"Here," she said, sliding her hands down his arms and pulling his wrists around her waist. "Let me help you."

Craig gulped. He certainly didn't need her help moving closer. Yet, she felt so damn good, her tiny waist warm under his loose grip. At this point, he might need a jolt of ten thousand electric volts just to keep him away.

When her fingers returned to his shoulders and traced underneath the opening of his collar, he offered one last warning. "What happens if you end up regretting this?"

"How will we know unless you kiss me?" she asked, her breath whispering against his lips.

Oh, hell. One little kiss wasn't going to hurt.

When he dipped his head to hers, pain was the last thing on his mind. In fact, finally kissing her felt like pulling into his driveway after months of being on the road. She opened her lips and her tongue tentatively reached out to his. Heat and urgency filled him and he drew her in closer and responded with his own tongue, more forceful and more exploratory.

Caroline pressed her small, lithe body

against his and every alarm inside him went off. This was too much. She was too much. Craig couldn't let things go any further. Breaking his lips away from hers was the easy part. Maintaining the distance and getting his breathing under control was way more difficult.

Well, that and trying to ignore the way Caroline's chest pressed against his as her lungs expanded with each of her little breaths. Her fingers were twisted into his collar and his hands were still cupped under her backside and he slowly dragged them back up to her waist.

Her cheeks were flushed and her lids appeared to be heavy since they were halfway closed as she studied his mouth.

"Are you okay?" he asked, more for himself than for her. He'd kissed plenty of women before, but none as responsive as her. Craig didn't know if he would ever be okay again.

"I think I felt something," she whispered and he tried not to take the words personally. He'd just felt his entire world burst out of the chute and she thought that perhaps she might've felt *something*? "But just to be sure, maybe you should kiss me again."

Compelled to make her feel more than just something, Craig lowered his head to hers again, then pulled back right before their lips met.

"Just one more," he murmured, needing all of his energy to fight this inner battle of self-control. The inner battle he was clearly already in danger of losing. "We can't go any further."

When he kissed her the second time, it was even better than the first. Their lips already knew how to move over each other's. Her mouth already knew how wide it needed to open to accept his probing tongue, and her hips knew just where to press against his, cradling his stiff arousal.

Caroline's fingers slipped into the open neck of his shirt, working the buttons loose as she slid her palms down his chest. His own hands were busy squeezing and massaging her rounded rear end, the silk fabric of her dress gathering together and lifting higher with each caress. The hem rose enough that the material no longer served as a thin barricade to the heat of her warm skin underneath. His thumbs traced the lacy edge of her panties and Caroline threw back her head and moaned.

His lips followed along her exposed neck down to her collarbone and her breath came in soft little pants. It took every ounce of strength Craig possessed to drag his mouth away from her a second time. Again, he moved his hands back up to her waist, but only because he was worried that if he completely let go of her, she would melt against him. Or he would melt against her. At this point it, his blood was pumping too fast to figure out where her body started and where his ended.

Also, by holding her this close, he didn't have to look at her eyes, didn't have to face the damage he might've inflicted. He drew in a ragged breath, resting his chin on top of her head. "We really should stop, honey."

Again, he hadn't meant to use the endearment, but he wasn't sorry for acknowledging the tender and protective feelings she evoked in him. Not that there weren't plenty of other things he could be sorry for.

She nodded, and when she lowered her arms, Craig stepped back to allow his body the opportunity to cool down, but then he was forced to observe her upturned face.

Instead of that dreamy expression she often

got when she was comfortable with him, the one where her eyes fluttered closed and her smile lit up the room, Caroline was staring at him like he'd just poisoned the herd's drinking water. Her eyes were huge and round and her mouth was frozen into a little O, as though she were in shock.

Oh, no. Had they gone too far? Had he pushed her too much? Was she completely disgusted by him? He hoped he wouldn't regret the answer, but he had to ask, "Caroline? Is everything okay?"

"Never better," she squeaked out in a hoarse voice before running to her bedroom and slamming the door closed.

Chapter 10

Caroline had absolutely no idea who that man was out in her living room, but he most definitely was *not* her fiancé.

Lying on her bed and staring blankly at her ceiling, Caroline touched her swollen lips. There was no way she could ever have forgotten what *that* felt like. After their first kiss, she was sure that she'd never kissed Craig Clifton before in her life. But she'd begged him to continue the make-out session just to confirm it, and it was during their second kiss that all of it came back to her. When he'd pulled his lips from hers, everything flooded into her mind at once.

Yet, instead of confronting him about any of it, she'd run straight to her bedroom and slammed the door closed. Twenty minutes later, she was still struggling to get her breathing under control.

They weren't engaged. Craig wasn't even her boyfriend. She'd been thinking about the words of Winona Cobbs when she first laid eyes on him two days ago. The images from that morning came back with the kind of clarity that can only be seen by events being replayed in slow motion. All the pieces finally clicked into place—the way she'd been balancing on that stupid chair, seeing him come into her office wearing that sexy tan cowboy hat, spotting the hook-shaped scar on his neck and, finally, the way the pink donut box went flying in the air as he ran toward her.

Engaged by Christmas. That was what she'd been thinking before knocking herself out. Had the doctor specifically said Caroline had suffered from amnesia, or was there another word she'd used? Reaching for the smartphone on her nightstand, she did some research online and read about an amnesia-like condition called confabulation.

So I made it all up? Caroline thought, staring at her screen. She heard the television in the living room go off and the sound of something bumping into a piece of wood furniture, followed by Craig's muffled curse. No, the man was completely real and currently getting ready to fall asleep on the other side of the wall, oblivious to the fact that Caroline had just remembered the truth.

Which brought everything back full circle. Obviously, she hadn't imagined Craig, but for some reason, she'd imagined that they were engaged. Yet why *him*? Why not Drew Strickland or his brother, Ben, both of whom were strangers and also in the office when she'd injured her head? Because neither one of them was Craig. It was as simple and as complicated as that.

Before Caroline had moved to Rust Creek Falls, she and some of her friends from the dorms had driven to town on a lark. Their favorite reality show, *The Great Roundup*, was being filmed nearby and the other girls wanted to be close to the action. Caroline had been coming out of the Ace in the Hole bar for a breath of fresh air when an older woman passed along the sidewalk. There'd been something familiar about her and it wasn't until the woman got to the corner of Buckskin Road that Caroline realized she was Winona Cobbs, the psychic from that nationally syndicated show Rita Rodriguez didn't approve of her daughter watching.

Caroline had caught up to Winona, not because she wanted to ask for a free reading or an autograph, but because the woman was walking with a slow limp and approaching a dark intersection. Caroline had asked the little old lady if she needed help crossing the road and when Winona took the offered arm, a strange expression had crossed her weathered face. Her eyes had grown bright and stared right through Caroline, like Dr. Robinson's penlight, trying to search for answers.

Winona's voice was lower in person than it had been on her shows, but it was just as authoritative when, without warning, she'd predicted, "You'll find what your heart is looking for here."

"Here?" Caroline had asked. "In Rust Creek Falls?"

The old psychic had nodded, but didn't explain what it was Caroline was looking for or how she would find it. "When?"

"Be patient, child," Winona had replied,

patting her gnarled, freckled hand against Caroline's. "It'll happen before you turn twenty-four."

"What will happen?"

"Your engagement."

The pronouncement had taken Caroline aback, but she'd always wanted to get married and knew with absolute certainty that a wedding was the thing her heart was looking for. She hadn't been able to keep the eagerness out of her voice when she asked, "To whom?"

"To the one with the pocket full of Life Savers and the three-legged cat that sleeps on both his pillows. Just remember, your cowboy is scarred for a reason, so be careful not to let him go."

But before Caroline could ask for more details, the other patrons had spilled out of the bar and Winona Cobbs was caught up in the crowd, leaving Caroline standing on the street corner, full of hope and unanswered questions.

Until Craig had walked into her office over two years later.

Actually, seeing him hadn't really answered anything. But, according to one of the brain injury articles Caroline had just read online, her concussion had forced her mind to fill in the blanks with what she'd wanted to see—that Craig was the scarred cowboy from Winona's prediction. Everyone in that hospital room when she'd finally awakened must have thought that she was completely nuts. Even Caroline could see how absolutely crazy it sounded for her to think she was engaged to a total stranger. It certainly explained why Josselyn and Drew and Craig had all stared at her that day as though she'd lost her mind.

However, the only thing Caroline couldn't explain was why any of them would go along with the whole charade in the first place. Especially Craig.

Throwing off the comforter, Caroline stood and walked to her bedroom door, determined to wake him up and ask him exactly that. Her hand gripped the knob and it took two tries to twist it open because her palms were so damp. She'd barely opened the door a crack when she saw the mound under the blankets on her sofa bed move. Then she heard his soft sigh as he nestled deeper into the thin mattress and something pulled at her heart.

Standing there frozen, Caroline was flooded

with another realization. If she went out there and admitted that she remembered they weren't truly engaged, there would no longer be a reason for Craig to stay and take care of her. Not that she really needed anyone looking out for her anymore, but if he left she would probably never see him again.

Not only had she made a complete fool of herself insisting that they were engaged, but then she'd doubled down on her belief by spouting all that stuff about a loving heart and the truest wisdom and trusting her instincts about a man who, in reality, was a total stranger.

In Caroline's defense, though, she'd suffered a head injury and had been relying on the very random mutters of an old psychic walking down the road late one night. Not that believing in fortune-tellers made her appear to be any more rational, but when Winona Cobbs had spoken those words, Caroline had felt the premonition all the way down to her bones.

She'd believed it way before she'd met Craig, and now that she'd kissed him, she knew it with even more certainty. It wasn't scientific, but being with him just felt right.

Besides, how else would she have known all those details about him? The pocket full of Life Savers, the three-legged cat, the sleeping with two pillows?

The scar?

The only part of Winona Cobbs's prediction that hadn't actually come true yet was Caroline being engaged by her twenty-fourth birthday—which was this Christmas.

Bracing her body between the small opening of the bedroom door and the frame, Caroline took several deep breaths as she contemplated her best course of action.

As much as she should admit the truth to Craig, she only had one more month to make him fall in love with her. Would it really be all that wrong to let him go on believing that they were engaged? Or that Caroline *thought* they were engaged?

She pressed her fingers to her pounding temples as she mentally sorted through all the confusion and her conflicting emotions. Caroline walked back to her bed, wishing she had someone to talk it over with. Someone who could make sense of it all.

Someone who could tell her how to keep the man she'd been destined to find.

* * *

The following morning, Craig was coming out of the shower when he heard Caroline talking in the kitchen.

"Oh, good, you're safe." Another female's voice echoed inside the small rental house and Craig froze in the doorway. He'd left his duffel bag in the living room and, having just slept in his boxers, the closest item of clothing he could shimmy into when Caroline came out of her room was a nearby pair of jeans, which was all he'd worn when he'd made a beeline for the bathroom earlier. If they had company, it would look pretty odd for Craig to walk out there bare-chested.

"It was just a concussion, Mom," Caroline replied and Craig eased away from his hiding spot behind the bathroom door. Her parents were out of the country, which meant they couldn't possibly be here at her house.

"We got your email, angel," a male baritone added to the conversation. "Who is this Craig fellow?"

She must have the speaker feature turned all the way up on her phone. His own father had once tried to show Craig how to do that so he wouldn't have to stop working anytime one of his brothers or sisters called, but he always hit the wrong button and ended up disconnecting the call.

"Oh. I forgot I mentioned him in the email," Caroline said as she walked to the edge of the kitchen, a mixing bowl cradled in one arm as she whisked some batter. She caught sight of Craig and gave him a tense smile before putting her forefinger to her lips in the universal sign to mean "Please keep quiet."

She didn't have to ask twice. The last headache Craig needed was for her parents to find out some stranger was lying to their daughter and shacking up with her. Luckily, they weren't there in person. Craig's nose twitched at the scent of freshly brewed coffee and the promise of the maple-pecan waffles Caroline had said she was making when she'd woken him up this morning.

"Are you really engaged?" her mom asked as Craig practically tiptoed toward his duffel bag, unsure of how much sound her cell phone could pick up.

"We don't even know him," her dad added.

"You're not cooking for him, are you?" her mom asked. "Did you know that in the Aka society in Africa, the men do all the cooking?

Many of the males even breastfeed the babies. Although, I suppose technically it would be suckling since they can't produce—"

"I like to cook, Mom," Caroline interrupted, thank goodness. Craig got to his duffel, only to discover that most of his clothes were missing.

Mrs. Ruth, or perhaps Dr. Ruth since she was a college professor, continued on about some pygmy tribe halfway across the globe and Craig tried to wave at Caroline to get her attention and ask where his shirts were. But her back was to him as she faced the stove.

Craig walked into the kitchen to whisper in her ear, and that was when he realized Caroline wasn't on speakerphone. Her laptop was propped on the counter and two very surprised people appeared on the screen facing him.

Oh, crap.

"He's real." Her dad was the first to speak.

"He's really *naked*," her mother replied, moving her reader glasses down her nose.

Craig looked behind him to judge the distance to the front door and tried to determine how cold it would be outside if he made a run for it. But Caroline shoved a cup of coffee into his hands before he could take off.

"Mom, you spent eight months in the Polynesian islands studying the history of ancient hula performances. You even made Dad dress in a loincloth."

"It wasn't a loincloth," her mother replied and Craig suddenly wished he would never have to hear the word *loincloth* again. "It was a ceremonial *malo* and it was a gift to your father from Professor Ka'ukai."

Caroline poured batter into the waffle iron on the opposite side of the stove as though making breakfast and video chatting with her parents about her half-naked fiancé was part of her normal Sunday morning routine. "My point is that you're well accustomed to seeing men without their shirts."

Too much information, Craig thought, resisting the urge to pull the cherry-printed apron off the sink and cover up.

"It's a pleasure to meet you, Dr. and Dr. Ruth," Craig offered weakly. Hopefully, nobody was appraising his chest for either breastfeeding suitability or hula-dancing capabilities.

"It's actually Dr. Ruth and Dr. Rodriguez," Caroline's father corrected with a wink. "We're not married."

Dr. Rodriguez then began a long lecture using phrases such as *female servitude* and *matrimonial bondage*, and Craig whispered out one side of his mouth to Caroline, "Where are my clothes?"

"I needed to run a load of laundry," she said, her lips equally tight.

"Did you say *laundry*, Caroline?" Her mom's face moved closer to the screen, as though the woman could hear better by looking more closely into the little webcam. "Please tell me that you're not already falling into the stereotypical gender roles that Western civilization has forced upon females as a means to exert the imbalance of power of a male-dominated society."

"I didn't ask her to do my laundry," Craig defended, one palm up as though he was being asked to swear on a stack of Bibles. "I normally do it myself."

"And he knows how to churn butter, too," Caroline added, making Craig glance at her sideways.

"Let them work out the distribution of domestic chores for themselves, Rita. It's still early in their engagement." Then the older man turned back to the screen. "And speaking of engagements, when our angel sent us an email mentioning some fiancé from out of the blue, we were a little worried, thinking we had our own Miss Havisham on our hands."

"Who's Miss Havisham?" Craig asked. There were a million ways this conversation should be steered, but he had no idea who was holding the reins. So he just tried to follow along.

"From *Great Expectations*?" her father said. "She's this old spinster woman who was jilted at the altar and goes around in her wedding gown—"

"Okay, Dad, I have to get to the office," Caroline interrupted quickly. But her father continued his dissertation as Craig's phone suddenly rang. Relieved for the excuse to get out of the kitchen, Craig quickly walked toward the coffee table.

Trying to mute his phone, he accidently swiped on the wrong button and his own mother's voice echoed on the speaker. "Craig? Are you there?"

"Hey, Mom," he said, looking for the button to switch off the speaker, but the entire display had gone black. Really? The one time he didn't want the feature to work was the one time he couldn't shut it down.

"I hear you're bringing a woman for Thanksgiving," Carol Clifton said, drawing Caroline's attention from her own parental inquisition.

"Word travels fast," Craig muttered. He was trying to push the circular home button on his phone, but it wasn't recognizing his thumbprint. Probably because his hands were so damn sweaty.

He heard more talking from the kitchen, where Dr. Ruth and Dr. Rodriguez were still visible on the laptop. Unfortunately, his mom heard the same thing.

"Oh, my gosh," his mother practically squealed. "Is that your new fiancée?"

Fiancée? That was more serious than the "lady friend" gossip Rob had mentioned. Craig glanced over his shoulder to make sure Caroline hadn't heard and then lowered his voice. "You know about that?"

"Oh, yeah. Ben Strickland told your brother Jonathan about it," his mom replied as though it was every day that one of her sons managed to find himself in the middle of a pretend engagement. "Put her on the phone."

"She's talking to her own parents right

now," Craig replied, running his fingers over his scalp and wondering if it would be worth catching pneumonia to go outside with wet hair.

"You guys aren't going to her folks' for Thanksgiving, are you? It's the first year in a long time that I'm gonna have all my kids at the house together."

"No, we can come there, Mrs. Clifton," Caroline said from behind him, apparently disconnected now from her own conversation.

"Fantastic," his mom replied. "Dear, I can't wait to meet you. Craig, make sure you stop by Daisy's on your way out of town and bring a pie."

His free hand dropped from his damp head to his neck as he tried to massage some of the tension away. "But I thought Meemaw was baking the pies."

"She is. However, Grandpac is also coming now and unless you want your new girlfriend to see a repeat of the Pecan Pie Controversy of 2011, you'll bring an extra one."

"I'd be happy to make a pie, Mrs. Clifton," Caroline volunteered. Craig pivoted to face his pretend fiancée and shook his head at her before it was too late.

"That might work as long as Meemaw doesn't know you made it yourself, dear. And please call me Carol. Or even Mom?"

Okay, his mother's tone was a bit too hopeful and Caroline's smile was a bit too pleased. Taking her to his family's ranch for Thanksgiving would all but seal their fate. It was entirely too risky.

Luckily, Craig still had a couple of days to get out of this mess. "Let's not finalize anything until later in the week, okay, Mom?"

"Sounds like a plan," his mom said and Craig wanted to reply that there was absolutely no plan. But the woman, who had raised eight children—and knew her way around the very best stall tactics—continued, "I'm guessing you two will be coming out on Wednesday? Everyone else is coming out on Wednesday."

"Probably Thursday morning, Mom," Craig sighed and Caroline smiled even wider.

"It's a long drive to Thunder Canyon from Rust Creek Falls, though. So don't be late."

Chapter 11

"Why couldn't I make the pie myself?" Caroline asked Thursday morning as she climbed into the passenger side of Craig's vehicle.

For the past three days, he'd insisted on driving her to and from work and he'd always held open the door.

"Remember I told you about making sure you don't take sides between Meemaw and Grandpac?" he asked, reaching across her legs to place the pink bakery box he'd picked up from Daisy's yesterday on the floorboard between them. It was the closest he'd gotten to her since the night they'd kissed.

Thousands of times this week, she'd been prepared to tell him that she'd regained her memory. But then he'd call her "honey," and her breath would bottle up in her lungs and all she could do was smile at him. Or he'd show up at her office, his boots and jeans all dusty from whichever local ranch he'd visited that day, and his concerned blue eyes and his sexy cowboy hat were a welcome sight after a long afternoon dealing with pushy vendors or mind-changing brides.

Then there was the morning when his brother had called him while they were in the truck. Craig's Bluetooth had automatically switched on and she heard Will ask if he and Caroline wanted to carpool to Thunder Canyon for Thanksgiving.

At that point, her curiosity became stronger than her guilt and she thought that meeting his family might give her some sort of insight about the man who'd established himself as her protector, while simultaneously keeping his distance from her. Maybe he wasn't as physically attracted to her as she was to him. This trip would give her the opportunity to find out.

Caroline reached for her seat belt. "And remember I told *you* that I can handle squabbling family members in my sleep? I do it at work all the time."

"That's the other reason I didn't want you to make the pie. You've been so busy at work and every night you come home and make me these fabulous home-cooked meals when you should be resting and taking it easy. Did you know that it can take weeks for a person to recover from a concussion?"

"I know." Caroline rolled her eyes and then sing-songed the same thing he'd been saying to her at least twice a day. "'Just because I can't see my injury doesn't mean it doesn't exist.'"

Normally, she would think it was sweet that he tried so hard to take care of her, but she was running on limited time here. She needed to impress him with her domestic abilities and get him to fall in love with her so that he'd propose before Christmas. But Craig seemed to be thwarting her attempts at every turn.

While she'd been working at Mikayla Brown's postbirth baby shower at Sunshine Farm on Sunday afternoon, he'd finished the laundry and ironed every single article of her clothing, including her sports bras, her hand towels and her Egyptian cotton bedsheets. On

Monday, he'd done the grocery shopping at Crawford's General Store while she'd been at the office, and on Tuesday, she'd come home to a spotlessly scrubbed bathroom.

Last night, he'd tried to grill rib eyes for her on her landlord's outdoor grill, but they'd run out of propane. And by the time he got back from the hardware store with a new tank, it was pouring rain and the wind was howling like crazy. She'd saved the meal by broiling the steaks and then wowing him with au gratin potatoes and her knowledge of useless college football stats.

If Craig needed a party thrown, Caroline had quite the résumé to show him. But Craig didn't seem to need anything. Or anyone. He certainly didn't need to kiss her again, she thought as he closed her door and climbed into the driver's side.

The sun was barely rising as they began the three-hundred-mile drive to Thunder Canyon. Since Craig didn't seem inclined to keep up any sort of conversation, Caroline turned on the radio. A blast of screaming electric guitar shot through the speakers, and her first instinct was to cover her ears.

But Craig raised the volume and then began

singing along with the heavy metal song. When he noticed her staring at him in shock, his voice trailed off. "What?"

"You mean, you purposely have this station programmed on your radio?"

"What else would I listen to?" he asked.

"Um, maybe country music? You're a cowboy."

"Oh, really?" He winked at her and a shiver ran down her spine. "I didn't get the memo."

They ended up compromising on a classic rock station and Caroline closed her eyes to prevent herself from chattering on senselessly. The past few nights that he'd stayed at her house, they'd settled into a routine of comfortable silence when the television was on or there was music playing, and she didn't want to do anything now that might rock the boat.

Or to remind her that she really had no business tagging along for a family holiday when they weren't really engaged. Yet.

That "yet" part was what gave Caroline an unprecedented bout of nausea. She would've liked to blame it on motion sickness but she'd never been carsick before in her life. It had to be her nerves telling her that this was a bad idea. Sure, his mom had invited her, but did his family really know the truth? That she and Craig had really only known each other a few days? On the other hand, if she didn't call him her fiancé or perpetuate this myth that they were in a legitimate relationship, then she wasn't technically deceiving anyone.

Plus, if she was being truly honest with herself, she really didn't want to spend Thanksgiving alone.

Halfway there, they pulled into a truck stop restaurant and gas station. Caroline used the restroom while Craig ordered them some breakfast sandwiches and coffee to go. The closer they got to Thunder Canyon, the more nervous Caroline's tummy became. Maybe meeting his parents and the rest of his family was a bad idea. After all, they'd been practically living together the last few days and not once had they socialized with any of his married siblings who lived nearby. Craig saw them while she was at work, but when he was with her, they didn't so much as go to the Gold Rush Diner to share a meal, let alone be seen anywhere out in public together.

Not that most of the people in Rust Creek Falls didn't already know there was something going on with them. But nobody seemed to know what that "something" was. In fact, a small group of ladies at the baby shower on Sunday had brought up his name with questions in their eyes, but Caroline had been in work mode and didn't think it would be professional to talk about her dating life. Or the fact that she and Craig had never truly gone on an actual date.

The irony was, the more nervous Caroline grew with each passing mile that brought her closer to lying directly to his family, the more relaxed Craig became. Okay, so maybe she wasn't exactly lying to his parents. Initially, she'd really thought she and Craig were engaged, and since he still hadn't corrected her, their engagement could be construed as a form of implied consent on his part. Perhaps he really *did* want to marry her.

Still, the fact remained that Craig had been quiet and tense during the first half of the drive. Yet now he began to speak more, pointing out landmarks and telling her a story about the creek where Grandpac had taken him and his brothers fishing when Craig had been in the sixth grade.

"Rob, my youngest brother, had been eager

to catch the biggest trout and didn't bother looking behind him before casting his line. We hear this shout, followed by a slew of four-letter words, but it was too late. Rob had got his hook caught in Grandpac's ear, then felt so bad about it he yanked the pole to try and pull it out. He ended up ripping right through the cartilage."

"Your poor grandfather!" Caroline shuddered.

"More like poor Jonathan. He's the second oldest and was closest to the first-aid kit when it happened. Grandpac cussed up a blue streak when Jonathan tried to disinfect the wound and bandage it up. Between you and me, I think that's why my brother became a pediatrician instead of going into geriatric medicine."

"So one of your brothers is a doctor?" Caroline turned in her seat. She recalled that day coming home from the hospital, when Craig had admitted that she hadn't met any of his family yet. So it wasn't like she had to pretend that she didn't know anything about his siblings. "Tell me about the others."

"Jonathan is married to Dawn, who is a nurse. Next is Will. We went to his and Jordyn's house that day…" Craig didn't have to say which day that was. She remembered. It was the same day she'd insisted that he come stay with her at her house.

"Got it." She tried to sound casual. "Who's next?"

"My sister Catherine and her husband, Cody, then Rob, who is single and still lives on the ranch. Cecelia is after him—she's married to Nick—then Calista and her husband, Jake. My sister Celeste, everyone calls her C.C., is the baby. Maybe I should've written it all down for you ahead of time."

"Craig, it's my job to remember who's who. We once planned a wedding for a bride with thirteen bridesmaids. To this day, I can tell you their dress sizes and whether their dates requested the prime rib or the salmon." Then Caroline proceeded to list the names of his siblings in order, along with their spouses. "I got this."

When he smiled at her across the cab of his truck, her throat constricted. It occurred to Caroline that she had never seen Craig smile so broadly. She'd seen looks of concern, looks of curiosity, even looks of desire. She'd even seen several grins. But she had never seen him as truly happy as he looked at that exact moment.

Apparently, his family was everything to him. Caroline really hoped she didn't blow this.

When they'd passed the turnoff to Interstate 90, Craig's blood had run cold at the sight of the wooden white cross on the side of the road.

It was why he hadn't said much to Caroline during the first half of the road trip. No matter how many times he'd driven the stretch of highway from Rust Creek Falls to Thunder Canyon, seeing that small handcrafted monument to one of his biggest failures always haunted him.

He hadn't brought a woman home to meet his family since Tina, and even then, he technically hadn't brought her home since she'd practically been there the whole time. In fact, it had been the opposite when she died. They'd been at a bar with some of her cousins outside Kalispell and returning to Thunder Canyon late at night. Craig had been sound asleep in the passenger side and Tina behind the wheel of her daddy's old Jeep, probably too exhausted to have even seen the stalled logging truck before it was too late.

After the crash, he'd been lost and hurt, his relationships with women more about filling a temporary physical need. But he could only ride bulls for so long before his body began reminding him that he was no longer in his prime. Eventually, Craig had been forced to go home to confront his past as well as the rest of life. The life he was now meant to have without Tina.

Craig liked to think that he'd made his peace with all of it. After all, he'd driven this exact same route hundreds of times before. But he'd never driven it with another woman. Fortunately, with each mile that separated him and that white cross, his guilt was slowly replaced with an eagerness to be home. To see his ranch and his family and his future.

By the time he and Caroline stopped for breakfast, Craig's muscles had lost most of their tension. And by the time they passed the sign welcoming them to Thunder Canyon, he was downright chatty. In fact, he felt like he'd been talking nonstop for the past twenty minutes while Caroline seemed to shrink against the passenger seat. His family was huge and overwhelming, and, of course, a city girl and an only child like Caroline—even if she could easily memorize and recite everyone's name—might be feeling out of her element.

He'd called his dad yesterday and spoken with all of his brothers, explaining Caroline's condition and urging them to just go along with the fake engagement. Craig knew better than to appeal directly to his mom and sisters. All of his female relatives would tell him that this was a horrible idea.

As if Craig wasn't already perfectly aware of that, thank you very much.

Still, what if someone in his family slipped and said something? Chances were that there was going to be a slew of people huddled on the front porch when they arrived, eager to meet her and bombard them both with questions. Perhaps he should gently prepare her for the fact that one of his relatives was likely to say something that might trigger her memory.

"So," he started, tapping his fingers against the steering wheel. "Your parents seemed a bit surprised that you were engaged."

Okay, so that wasn't exactly what he'd wanted to bring up. He was still trying to be cautious about not adding any undue stress on her, but he wanted her to understand that his family, too, might have a similar response. They might exhibit the same kind of curiosity to this unexpected engagement of theirs.

"They *did* seem surprised," Caroline replied, but didn't add any theories on why that might be.

"Are you feeling sick?" he asked and she followed his eyes to where her palms rested against her stomach.

She yanked her hands away quickly, then fiddled with the strap on her seat belt. "I guess I'm just a little nervous."

"It's not too late to turn back," he offered even as he made a right onto the long driveway that would lead to his family's ranch house.

"No," she said, turning in her seat toward him, her brown eyes full of determination. "Don't turn back. I really do want to be here."

She also thought she wanted to marry him. And the longer he let her go on believing that, the more attached she would get. Even *he* was getting a little too comfortable in this alternate universe they'd inadvertently created. The problem was that when she finally remembered that he wasn't the man she thought he was, this carefully constructed bubble of theirs would burst. It was like chewing gum. The bigger the bubble got, the bigger the mess it would make when it finally exploded in his face.

But that didn't stop him from continuing down the gravel road toward his home.

Despite all the vehicles parked in the circular drive, Craig had been wrong about his prediction of everyone waiting on the front porch to greet them. In fact, when they got out of his truck, the only member of their welcoming committee was an old tomcat sunning himself on the front steps and watching their approach with equal parts mild interest and total disdain.

"You really do have a three-legged cat." Caroline shifted the pie box into the crook of her left arm and slowly approached the porch, holding out an open palm to the normally cantankerous feline. He was surprised the old grouch was allowing a stranger to pet him.

Craig reached out to scratch the tabby between the ears but was suitably rejected in favor of Caroline's ministrations. He stood back up, knowing the cat could only ignore him for so long.

"Yep, and he always punishes me like this whenever I've been away from the ranch. Don't you, Tiny Tim?"

The box wobbled against Caroline's hip and she set it down on the wooden step. "Wait, your cat's name is Tiny Tim?"

"Yeah, but he's obviously not very tiny, are you, boy?" The tabby finally purred at Craig before nudging its chin against his leg. "He also doesn't have the same sunny disposition as his namesake."

"His namesake?" she asked and Craig bent down to rub Tim's back when he realized Caroline's hand wasn't moving.

"I know what you're thinking, that it's not very politically correct to name a three-legged cat after the kid from that Scrooge movie. But my sister C.C. was the one who came up with it and since she was only seven at the time and already spoiled rotten, we never really corrected her."

"It's called *A Christmas Carol*," she offered, her eyes wide with disbelief.

"What is?"

"That Scrooge movie you're talking about. It's actually a book by Charles Dickens. I'm named after that story."

The hairs along the nape of his neck stood up and Craig's hand paused in midair above Tim's pointy ears. Not wanting to acknowledge the coincidence, he replied casually, "That's right. I remember that night. You told me you were named after a Dickens book. But later on, your dad mentioned something about a Miss Havisham."

"No, that was just my dad's way of making a joke about my love for wedding dresses. Wait." She stood up straighter on the step above him. "Of all the things you remember from *that* night, me babbling on about my name is what stands out the most?"

"Not the most." He rose to his full height, unable to resist coming face-to-face with her and meeting her challenge. There was something about being on his own property, in his own element, that made Craig finally feel as if he was on solid footing. "I also remember every single sigh you made as you kissed me to within an inch of my control."

Color flooded Caroline's cheeks, but she didn't back away. Instead, she lifted her hands to the back of his neck and pulled him closer. "Maybe this time I can make you lose all your control."

Her lips had just met his when the unmistakable sound of his grandfather's truck horn blared through the yard.

Chapter 12

"You must be the little filly Craig plans on marrying," an older, heavyset gentleman said as he lumbered up the porch steps. Caroline's response was immediately muffled against the shoulder of the newcomer's tobacco-scented sheepskin coat as he swept her into a bear hug.

"Grandpac, you're gonna suffocate my fiancée before anyone else gets to meet her," Craig said from behind her.

"So you're sayin' I'm the first to welcome her to the family?" the man asked as he pumped a triumphant fist in the air, thereby loosening his grip while keeping one beefy arm planted around her shoulders. "So, when's the wedding?"

Caroline opened her mouth to explain they still had time to figure all of that out, but then she flashed back to her earlier vow to not say anything that might mislead his family. She aimed her tight-lipped smile at Craig so he could field this particular question.

"We haven't set a date yet," Craig replied vaguely, just as he'd done that day she'd been released from the hospital. And just like then, he looked at something off in the distance, probably so he wouldn't have to make eye contact with anyone. While Caroline was relieved to see that he seemed uncomfortable with playing fast and loose with the truth, her muscles also relaxed at his nonanswer. She didn't want to be complicit in any blatant lies.

"Well, as soon as it happens, I want to be the first to know." The older Clifton released his hold on Caroline so he could pull his grandson into an equally enthusiastic bear hug.

"The first to know what?" The front screen door slammed behind a woman with silver hair cut into a sleek bob. She was shorter than Caroline and wore a two-piece velvet tracksuit in a bright purple color that clashed with the turkey-printed dish towel cinched around her still-trim waist. There also appeared to be rhinestone letters spelling out something across the seat of her pants, but Caroline couldn't see the word from this angle.

"Happy Thanksgiving, Meemaw." Craig had to push against his grandfather's elbow to slip out of what looked to be a hearty and somewhat territorial embrace. He then gave his grandmother a hug and the smaller—and possibly stronger—woman didn't allow him to pull away either until he gasped, "I want to introduce you to Caroline."

"I already met her." Grandpac's barrel chest puffed out as Meemaw passed by him. "Before anyone else."

"You don't count, you ol' grizzly bear." The woman flicked her wrist at the older man before also pulling Caroline into a tight hug. Caroline's ribs threatened to snap in half. Yep, Meemaw was definitely the stronger of the two grandparents. Craig's grandmother whispered in Caroline's ear, "Just ignore him. I always do."

At least, she'd tried to whisper. Unfortunately, she didn't seem to realize how loud her voice was.

"I heard that," Grandpac called out. "Instead of wasting all that money on a new hearing aid that doesn't work, you should've invested in another one of your fancy cruises for single seniors. In fact, I'll pay for it myself if it means I can send you halfway around the world and get you outta my hair once and for all."

"What hair?" Meemaw rose onto her tiptoes as she knocked the sweat-stained cowboy hat off his forehead, exposing a shiny bald head. Then the older woman winked at Caroline as she sauntered toward the door. "Come on inside, you two. I'm gonna cut into my famous pecan pie so we can have a little dessert before dinner."

"The only thing that pie is famous for is a bad case of constipation," Grandpac muttered before bending down to retrieve his Stetson. But Caroline noticed the way the older man's sparkling blue eyes—the same color as Craig's—remained riveted on Meemaw's backside. When he rose, Grandpac slapped his hat against his thigh and stomped past them in full pursuit. He was barely stepping inside the house when he shouted, "And why in the hell does it say 'DIVA' across your rear end, woman?"

"So those are my grandparents," Craig said, hands planted on his hips as he rocked back on his boot heels.

"I think they're adorable." Caroline smiled.

"Well, everyone else thinks they're insufferable."

"Insufferable relatives are my specialty, remember?" She looped her arm through his and patted his muscular forearm, trying not to think of the way it had felt wrapped around her waist a few moments ago. "Don't worry. This isn't my first rodeo."

When it came time to eat the Thanksgiving meal, there was a brief skirmish between the grandparents as they fought over who got to sit next to Caroline. In the end, Craig's sister Catherine had to ask her husband, Cody, to scoot down a spot to accommodate Meemaw, and Caroline found herself sandwiched right in between the two bickering seniors.

Calista and Jake sat across from them, and poor Dawn, Jonathan's wife and a registered nurse, got stuck on the other side of Grandpac and was forced to endure endless questions about his new blood pressure medication, his elevated cholesterol levels and whether

Meemaw's store-bought biscuits contained more saturated fat than Cecelia's crescent rolls.

"Whose biscuits are you calling store-bought, you ol' sourpuss?" Meemaw leaned forward, glaring over her crystal goblet.

"Is that your fifth or your sixth glass of wine, Doris?" he replied.

"You two need to knock it off," Carol Clifton called out from the head of the table. Caroline was relieved someone was trying to smooth the waters between the two feisty elders, because Craig was at the opposite end with Rob and C.C. and Will, pretending to be in a deep discussion about the vaccination schedules for calves. Fakers.

"Not that I would know where she gets her biscuits," Grandpac said under his breath to Caroline. "I wouldn't eat anything that woman put before me."

"Looks to me like you don't really discriminate about where your food comes from." Meemaw reached around Caroline and poked a finger right into Grandpac's generous belly.

"I know you normally have a hard time keeping your paws off me, lady, but you really need to control yourself in front of the kids." Grandpac swatted his napkin at the older woman's hand.

Meemaw's reflexes were too quick, though, and she snatched a corner of the orange linen cloth. Caroline plastered a smile on her face and stood up, using her body to break up their impromptu game of tug-of-war.

"Mr. Clifton, your sweet potato casserole is looking a bit cold. Why don't I go pop that in the microwave for you?"

Jordyn, Will's wife, had already reheated the man's plate when he'd complained that the gravy Meemaw made was coagulating. But when Caroline made the offer, several gasps sounded throughout the dining room and everyone's attention shifted to the chair Caroline had just vacated.

Nick, Cecelia's husband, appeared at her side and whispered, "Go. Save yourself. I'll slip into your seat and try to keep them separated for as long I can. The new in-law always gets Wall Duty at their first family dinner, and so far, you've lasted longer than any of us did our first go-rounds."

Luckily, Craig grabbed the empty bowl of mashed potatoes and followed her into the kitchen. It gave Caroline the opportunity to ask, "What is Wall Duty?"

"It's the person who ends up with the unfortunate task of being a literal barrier between my grandparents so they don't physically attack each other. They've never actually come to blows, so no need to look concerned. Although, it got real close that year when Grandpac allegedly fed Meemaw's secret recipe stuffing to her Yorkshire terrier."

"Allegedly?" Caroline asked, punching in the numbers on the microwave.

"Nobody actually saw him do it, but when Scruffins puked all over my dad's favorite recliner, Grandpac suggested it was proof that Meemaw's cooking wasn't fit for dogs, let alone human consumption." Craig used a wooden spoon to heap more potatoes into the serving dish. "Anyway, sorry you got put in the middle of the two of them. My family does it to all the new members as a sort of initiation, but let me know if it gets to be too much for you."

Something burst inside Caroline's chest as she followed Craig out of the kitchen, feeling about as warm and gooey as the yams and melted marshmallows on the plate she carried back to his grandfather.

She'd gotten Wall Duty. That meant his family had accepted her as one of its newest members.

"So tell me more about this amnesia of yours," Rob said to Caroline when Craig finally sneaked the remote control away from a sleeping Grandpac.

"Rob." Craig's voice issued a warning to his little brother. It was after dinner and several of his siblings had already left to return to Rust Creek Falls, but those were the ones who'd arrived the day before and hadn't already made a five-hour drive this morning. The thought of climbing back into his truck so soon for the return trip brought a throbbing ache to Craig's upper spine.

So far, most of his family had been pretty good about just going along with the flow and not asking Caroline any personal questions. Granted, it had helped to have his grandparents' constant quarreling as a diversion most of the day. But now that it was late in the afternoon and things were quieting down, some of his more daring siblings were getting a bit bolder in their curiosity.

"What do you want to know?" Caroline's

smile was pleasant, but they were sitting so close to each other on the sofa, Craig could feel her muscles tense.

"Why don't I put on the football game?" he said, trying to distract everyone from the direction of the conversation. But his fingers were a bit too overeager and he pressed the wrong channel.

Goldie Hawn's face popped up on the screen instead.

"Oh, hey," his sister C.C. said, coming into the living room. "I love this movie."

"I don't think I've ever seen it," Caroline replied, leaning forward to hear whatever the actress was saying to Kurt Russell.

"It's about this rich lady that hires a guy to do some work on her yacht, but doesn't pay him. Then the woman falls overboard, knocking herself out and waking up in the local hospital with amnesia. The worker guy needs someone to watch his kids and clean his house and figures since she still owes him money, he should pretend to be her husband and…" C.C.'s eyes widened as she trailed off, then wrestled the remote out of Craig's grip. "Actually, isn't there a college bowl game on right now?"

But C.C.'s words hung in the air and Caroline apparently was no longer interested in football because Craig could feel her narrowed gaze studying him. Of all the movies that had to be playing, it had to be one about tricking someone who was suffering from amnesia.

Luckily, Meemaw chose that exact moment to walk into the room. "Who wants to play gin rummy?"

"Deal me in," Grandpac said, slapping his hands together. He'd been snoring, but at the sound of his nemesis's challenge to a card game, he suddenly rose from the recliner like a bifocal-wearing phoenix rising from the ashes to reclaim his glory.

"Okay." Meemaw scanned her remaining grandchildren as though she were a general choosing which soldiers to lead into battle. "Craig, you and Rob can be on the old fart's team. I'll take C.C. and Caroline."

"All right." Caroline began to stand up, but both Craig and Rob grabbed onto an elbow and pulled her back down between them.

"Actually, I was going to take Caroline outside and show her around the ranch." Craig congratulated himself on the quick thinking even though he doubted someone like Caroline, with her impractical heels and her wispy dress, would want to go traipsing around the stables.

"At this hour?" Grandpac argued. "It's too dad-gum dark to see anything out there right now. You can show her around tomorrow."

"But we're going back to Rust Creek Falls tonight," Craig said.

"No, you're not," C.C. replied. For being the youngest of eight kids, his baby sister had no problem bossing everyone else around. "You're too tired and you've been rubbing your neck for the past hour."

"My neck's fine," Craig insisted, trying not to rotate it to stretch out the muscles.

"There's no way you're leaving me and C.C. alone to play cards with the grandparents." Rob leaned behind Caroline to whisper to Craig. Then his brother winked before raising his voice for everyone to hear. "I know senior citizens like you need their sleep, but stop being such an old fuddy-duddy, Craig."

"Fuddy-duddy?" Craig lifted an eyebrow.

"How old are you, Caroline?" Rob asked.

"Robert Clifton, you know better than to ask a lady her age." Meemaw flicked her dish towel against the back of his brother's head and Craig felt a brief moment of satisfaction.

Yet Rob pressed on. "All I'm saying is that if Craig is gonna go around robbing the cradle with a much younger—and much prettier—fiancée, then he should act like he isn't too old and broken down to actually fill a cradle when it comes time."

Meemaw smacked at Rob's head again and C.C. asked, "What do you mean 'fill a cradle'?"

"I believe they're talkin' about baby making," Grandpac volunteered, making the situation worse.

Caroline's cheeks blazed pink, and C.C., who was only a year younger than Craig's supposed fiancée, made gagging sounds. "Ew, gross."

"Making babies is a normal part of life," Meemaw told her youngest granddaughter. "Maybe if you went on one of those singles cruises with me you could find a nice gentleman to make babies with."

"Pish," Grandpac said with a shudder. "C.C., don't you dare go on a cruise with this man-hunting, she-devil grandmother of yours. She'll set you up with one of her wrinkly geriatric boyfriends. The kinda guy who'll buy you a cemetery plot right next to theirs for your wedding gift. Better to be a cradle robber like Craig than a grave robber like your Meemaw."

Craig wanted to draw Caroline to him and tuck her head against his shoulder so he could shield her from this humiliating conversation. And prevent her from hearing the repeated reminder of their age difference. But when he stretched his arm behind her, he realized she was shaking with silent laughter. Craig groaned. "Can everyone just stop talking about cradles and filling them?"

Meemaw pulled a deck of cards out of her purple velvet pocket. "I can as soon as you guys get your butts to the table and we start playing."

Chapter 13

Carol's and Rudy Clifton's faces both jerked up from their newspapers when Caroline and the other five entered the recently cleared dining room.

"Oh, no," Carol muttered, her eyes darting to the playing cards in her mother's hand.

Laughter bubbled inside Caroline's chest as she realized why Craig and Rob had been so quick in their efforts to stop her from agreeing to this game. Apparently, everyone else in the house felt the same way. However, she'd never been a part of a big family game night and surely all the Cliftons were overreacting about the ferociousness of Meemaw and Grandpac's constant competiveness.

"Guess those Black Friday deals aren't gonna shop themselves." Craig's dad stood up so quickly, his chair fell over backward. "Better head out to the stores now."

"Whoa." C.C. put out both of her palms. "You two have never been Black Friday shopping a day in your lives."

"So then we'll get a jump start on our Cyber Monday deals," Mr. Clifton replied.

Rob rolled his eyes. "It's still Thursday, Dad."

"Back in your seats," Craig commanded his mom and dad before using his thumb to gesture toward Meemaw and Grandpac. "They're *your* parents. If we have to play cards with them, then so do you."

When everyone moved to the opposite side of the table, Caroline decided to take matters into her own hands and suggested that they play with four teams and then orchestrated it so that the grandparents were paired together. Craig gaped at her like she was absolutely insane.

"Trust me," she whispered to him as his dad shuffled the cards. And when Meemaw and Grandpac won the first hand, everyone else relaxed and they were able to sit back and enjoy the game.

At least, it was relaxing until Rob had to leave to go check on the timer for the sprinklers in the south pasture and C.C. had to write a term paper and Mrs. Clifton told Craig that there was no way he was going to be driving back to Rust Creek Falls this late at night.

"I'll be fine." Craig stood, then held out his hand toward Caroline as though she needed his help to rise. Or maybe it was just his way of signaling to her that it was time to go.

"You of all people should know better than to risk it when you're this worn-out." His mom gave him a pointed look and even the grandparents disappeared. Quietly.

A pained expression crossed Craig's face and his jaw hardened to a rigidity Caroline had never seen on him before. Not that she knew him well enough to be an expert on his moods.

What she *did* know, though, was that even with his grandparents' perpetual squabbling—which she was pretty sure was mostly a ruse to gain attention from their grandchildren—she'd never had a better Thanksgiving. His huge family was loyal and hardworking and loving and everything she'd ever wanted to be a part of. However, if Craig was determined to leave, then she would stand by him.

"I can drive if you really want to go home tonight." Caroline placed her arm on his biceps, which was even more rigid than his jaw.

"Out of the question," Craig gritted out.

Caroline got the feeling that his determination didn't have anything to do with her head injury, yet, as an outsider, she wasn't sure what it was. Something wasn't right and she couldn't fix the problem unless she understood the source. And she wouldn't understand the source unless she got Craig to relax and tell her what was wrong.

All that muscle clenching was apparently taking its toll because Craig reached behind his neck and pressed three fingers to the base of his scalp. Since they were standing side by side, he must not have seen Caroline's hand lift up, causing him to give a slight jolt when she began to massage his neck. But at least he didn't move away. Taking that as a good sign, she stepped in front of him, forcing him to look at her.

"Honey," she started, smiling encouragingly at him until she had his undivided attention. "I'm fine with staying the night here."

"Don't you need to work tomorrow?" he asked, a muscle ticking along his upper jaw.

"I have the day off."

"But you didn't pack an overnight bag."

"She can borrow something from C.C.," his mom said from behind Caroline. "I'll go get some stuff now."

"See, I can borrow something from your sister," Caroline repeated, wanting Craig to understand that she was truly fine with staying the night. Rudy followed his wife out of the dining room, leaving Caroline and Craig alone.

Some of the tension eased from Craig's face and he lowered his voice to a whisper to ask Caroline, "But where will you sleep?"

Caroline thought she'd been in control until that point. Heat flooded her body and she licked her lips.

"She can sleep in your room," Meemaw said, coming out of the kitchen with the pink bakery box from Daisy's. "Anyone want more pie?"

Even though they were "engaged" and it was no secret that Craig had been shacking up with Caroline at her tiny rental house, Craig's mom knew the truth and insisted on her oldest son giving Caroline his room and sleeping in Jonathan and Will's old bedroom.

It was really for the best, Craig thought, staring blankly at the shelf containing Will's 4-H trophies and Jonathan's science fair award. Caroline fitted in so perfectly with his family and it had been all he could do to keep his hands off her since that interrupted kiss on the front porch this morning. But then Rob had gone and made that joke about robbing the cradle and Craig's pride—as well as his prior aches and pains—had flared up, and suddenly, he'd never felt more like an old man. An old man who was taking advantage of a much younger, much more naive woman. A woman who was under the mistaken belief that he planned to marry her.

The truth was, Craig didn't plan to marry anyone. He'd had his shot at the perfect partner with Tina, but all of that had crashed around him. Literally.

Seeing Caroline at his family's ranch only served to remind him that she was too young, too feminine, too citified to ever suit this life. Working on a ranch required commitment and strength and hard work and… and…

proper footwear. Did the woman even own a pair of boots?

Granted, she didn't buckle under the pressure of his grandparents. However, Caroline was a tiny, dainty thing with a closet full of high heels and a bathroom full of beauty products. She had to be miserable being stuck out on a ranch in the middle of nowhere. Not to mention meeting his entire family must've been a total overload for her recovering memory. He was supposed to be keeping things calm for her so her head injury could heal, not bringing more chaos into her life.

If she'd had her tiny little European car here, she probably would've been gunning its four-cylinder engine down the driveway the second Rob had called him a fuddy-duddy. Actually, probably well before then—like when his elderly grandparents practically knocked each other over in their race to get the seat next to Caroline at the dinner table.

Craig scratched his head, wondering if he could actually use his boisterous and pushy family to his advantage. Perhaps the more time she spent here, the sooner Caroline would come to the conclusion that they were worlds apart. That they were never meant to be together.

Although, she *had* been so diplomatic and understanding with his ornery grandparents when she didn't have to be. Then she'd been helpful to his parents in the kitchen when she could've just sat back and been a guest. Caroline had also demonstrated complete ease with his siblings and their spouses, asking them questions about their jobs and their hobbies.

Another thought took root. As an experienced party planner, perhaps Caroline had simply switched into professional mode and spent the day dealing with his family as though it was some sort of pro bono requirement. It was hard to read someone else's thoughts when they didn't even know their own mind. Maybe she'd been miserable the entire time.

Regardless of whether it was all a performance on her part, the fact remained that Craig had invited her here. He was supposed to be acting as her host and he couldn't fall asleep if he kept pacing around his brothers' room all night, worried about her discomfort. Opening the door, he peeked out to see if everyone else had already gone to bed. Pulling off his boots, he hoped his socks muted his footsteps on the old squeaky floorboards as he sneaked down the hallway.

Craig lightly tapped on the door to his own bedroom and when Caroline opened it, he sucked in his breath. Not that she looked breathtakingly sexy with her hair pulled into a high ponytail and dressed in a borrowed pair of pajamas covered with dancing pugs in Santa hats. No, his lungs refused to work because she was giving him that wistful smile again, the one that looked so happy. So comfortable. So confident that he couldn't possibly stay away from her.

Instead of asking her how she was, he stepped over the threshold and placed his hands on either side of her face, leaning down to claim the kiss that had been interrupted this morning when they'd first arrived.

As his lips melded to hers, he felt her arm against his waist before hearing the lock behind him click into place. Craig had been so absorbed in the taste of her, he'd lost all foresight to keep this late-night meeting private. That was the thing about Caroline—she knew things about him and she knew what he wanted, without even asking him.

He finally pulled away, studying her face for any signs of discomfort. Her eyelids were heavy and her lips were full and swollen, a hint of a smile still playing at their corners. His pulse picked up tempo and he had to command his hands to keep her at an arm's distance until he could get his breathing under control.

"Before I went to bed," he started, then made the mistake of glancing over her shoulder and toward the foot of his own queen-size mattress. The hammering in his heart spread to his lower extremities, and he had to shake his head and clear his mind before he could continue what he was saying. "I just wanted to check and make sure you were comfortable in here. Is there anything you need?"

With her face turned up to his and her eyes focused on his mouth, she tugged her lower lip between her teeth, then released it. "Only you."

Craig groaned and pulled her against him. The next kiss was deeper than the first and in that loose pajama shirt, it was easy for his hands to slip underneath the hem.

Just for a second. He would only let his work-calloused palms stroke the intoxicating silkiness of her skin for a second. But it wasn't enough time.

Just another inch. He would only move his thumbs up another inch. But then the rest of his fingers followed suit and he was splaying his hands on either side of her rib cage.

Just hold still. He wouldn't go any further. In fact, now was the time he should stop this maddening kiss, as well. But Caroline dragged her head away first, breaking her lips apart from his long enough to pull the pajama top over her head.

Just make her yours already. It was his last thought before he totally consumed her. His mouth slanted over hers, coaxing her tongue deeper inside so that he could suckle it.

She wasn't wearing a bra and, while he hadn't been able to get a good view of her chest before she'd immediately plastered her body against his, her rounded breasts easily filled his hands and her nipples tightened into tiny buds against his palms.

Caroline's soft little moans increased and he felt her pulling against his belt buckle. Anticipation raced through him as she got the first button of his fly undone. When the backs of her warm fingers dusted the tip of his erection, an electric current shot through him.

Craig was trying to shrug out of his own shirt when a deep, scratchy meow sound stopped him cold. His head whipped up and he saw Tiny Tim using his sole front paw to claw, press and reshape the stacked pillows on his bed. "What's my cat doing in here?"

"Well, this is *his* room, isn't it?" Caroline looked over her shoulder at the overweight tabby, who was now pacing in circles around the comforter and scowling at them. "He looks pretty mad at us for waking him."

"Actually, he looks like that when he's happy, too. But I think you're right about his level of annoyance at this moment. He's not used to having a lot of late-night activity going on in his bedroom." Then Craig winced at his own implication. Only an old fuddy-duddy would admit to going to bed alone every night with his cat.

"Maybe we should move to your brothers' room and let Tiny Tim get his sleep." Caroline's thumbs were still hooked above the fly of his jeans, her breathing still shallow.

It took every last drop of strength he possessed to encircle her wrists and drag her hands away. "Honey, we can't."

"Do you not want to?" she asked, staring at him with such a deep longing, Craig felt completely exposed. "Or is it that you don't want to right now?"

"I think you just felt how much I want to," he replied before buttoning his jeans back up so that the evidence of his desire wasn't further tempted. "But when I make love to you, I want you to know who I am."

"So you're saying that as soon as I remember, you'll finally make love to me?"

If you still want me to, he thought. But all he said was "Yes."

She sighed and backed away, but there was a promise glinting in her eyes. As he walked back to his brothers' room, he wondered if he'd just made a deal with the devil.

Because if Caroline Ruth finally learned the truth and she still wanted him, Craig would do much more than make love to her.

Chapter 14

"I think I may be in way over my head," Caroline confided to the palomino in the stall before her. She'd already admitted as much a few hours ago to Tiny Tim—who'd ignored Craig's commands to follow him down the hall to a different room last night. The cat clearly regretted his choice in bedmates because after hours of Caroline's tossing and turning and talking out loud about what she should say to her pretend fiancé, Tim began scratching at the door, demanding to be let outside well before dawn.

But at least the cranky tabby had led her

to the stables, where there were more pairs of triangle-shaped ears to listen to Caroline's venting. Obviously, she knew the animals couldn't really understand her, but growing up, she'd moved too often to keep a pet and she'd never had a sibling to use as a sounding board. She'd always been able to talk out her problems with her parents, then with her sorority sisters and, more recently, with her boss, Vivienne. But none of them were currently around, so these new four-legged friends—or three-legged in Tiny Tim's case—would have to do.

Caroline stroked the horse's silky blond muzzle as she went on. "I mean, how embarrassing and frustrating that he got me all worked up like that last night. And then he simply walked away, leaving me breathing all funny and wanting more."

The horse snorted in response.

"I know," Caroline continued. "You get it. You've probably had a stallion or two come sniffing around your stall. Maybe nipping you in the neck to get your attention. What I wouldn't have given for a good neck nip last night. Anyway, this might sound totally human of me, but this attraction I'm feeling for him? It's more than just the physical. I'm worried that if I lose him, I'll also lose all of this."

The mare's soulful brown eyes followed Caroline's arm as she gestured toward the rest of the ranch outside. She wanted Craig, but she also wanted the holiday dinners with all of the Cliftons and her own children carrying on their family's legacy. She didn't know it twenty-four hours ago, but his perfectly happy home out in Thunder Canyon, Montana, contained the entire life she'd always envisioned for herself and didn't know existed.

"I was trying to seduce him last night, I'll willingly admit that." At least, Caroline would admit that to a stable full of animals who couldn't reveal her secret. "But only because I was hoping to make him want me as much as I want him. Instead, all of his damn restraint and chivalry are now only making me fall harder for him."

The horse gave a little whinny, throwing back her nearly white mane and stomping her forelegs, probably in a show of sisterly solidarity.

"You're wearing jeans." Craig's voice surprised her and she caught her toe on the lower rung as she hopped down from the stall. The sun was starting to rise outside and his gaze traveled over her in the dim light, making her shudder in excitement. "And boots."

"Thanks for the warning," she whispered into her new friend's fury neck before turning toward Craig. "C.C. loaned everything to me."

"Everything except for the jacket," he replied, using his chin to gesture at the coat made of faux red leather with faux fur lining.

Caroline pulled it closer around her torso, feeling like a complete faux herself. She wished she had brought suitable attire with her to the ranch so it didn't appear as though she was overplaying the roles of both fiancée *and* cowgirl.

"I saw it on the hook by the back door and assumed it was your sister's, as well."

"Nah, Meemaw just thinks she's of a similar age as you and C.C. and shops accordingly."

Caroline's steps faltered as she thought about the way Craig's body had stiffened beside her last night when his brother Rob had made the joke about him robbing the cradle. She'd never really given his age any thought, but it was interesting that she and his so-called "baby sister" were only a year apart.

Yet, as she approached him, Craig stared at her legs encased in the tight denim as though he wasn't thinking of either his sister or grandmother at that exact second. A jolt of hope surged in Caroline's veins and she asked, "Why are you looking at me like that?"

"I guess I'm not used to seeing you in anything but skirts and dresses and high heels," he replied, rubbing the scar along his neck. "You almost look like you could fit in here."

"Almost?" Seeing the dark circles under his eyes put a little more swagger into her walk. Not that she wanted to see him exhausted, but it was somewhat of a relief to know they were both on a level playing field as far as lust-filled sleep deprivation went.

"I mean, we'd have to get you on a horse to really be sure." He smiled and she wondered if he was hoping to avoid any conversations about how hot and heavy things had gotten between them last night.

Recklessness coursed through her and she rested a hand on a jutted-out hip. "Is that an invitation to ride?"

"You actually want to go for a ride? On a horse?"

"Show me where you keep the saddles."

Caroline followed Craig to the tack room and looked at the rows of reins and bits hanging from the walls. This ranch operation of theirs was definitely bigger than she'd first thought. If she wanted to get to know the man, then she really needed to get to know all aspects of him, including his land. A little thrill of excitement shot through her.

But it sputtered to a halt when he patted a leather horn. "This one should fit you okay."

"It's a Western saddle, though." She pulled her bottom lip between her teeth as she studied her choices. Sure, the one Craig had picked out was smaller than most of the others, but it was still huge. Maybe she'd gotten a little too cocky when she'd suggested going for a ride. "Do you have an English one by any chance?"

"Wait." Craig did a double take in her direction. "You know the difference?"

"My parents were at Oxford when I was eight and then again when I was fourteen. I took equestrian lessons both times."

Craig studied her before finally hefting

the smaller saddle onto his shoulder. "Trust me. Since we're not doing any show vaults or playing polo today, you're gonna want the bigger one to distribute your weight."

"And do you have a horse in mind for me to ride?" Caroline asked as she picked up a plaid-patterned saddle blanket and followed him out of the tack room.

"I figured you'd want to take Marley out this morning. Looked like you two were pretty deep in conversation when I walked in."

Despite the low temperatures outside, heat filled Caroline's cheeks. *Lord, please tell me Craig was too far away to hear what I was saying to the mare.*

But the only answer was his boots crunching along the straw-covered concrete. With his arm lifted high to balance his load, the hem of his work jacket rose above the waistband of his worn jeans, exposing his well-muscled rear end.

That's it, she thought, racing across the stable floor to catch up with him. From now on, Caroline would have to always stay one step ahead of him. She was supposed to be the seducer, not the seducee. There was no way she was going to let this man and his perfectly shaped cowboy butt ride in front of her.

Craig tried not to watch the way Caroline's hips rocked in the saddle as she cantered along the trail in front of him. However, after a sleepless night with nothing but some unfulfilled fantasies to keep him company, he couldn't think of anything but his attraction to her.

Well, his attraction to her *and* her age. Rob's cradle-robbing comment from yesterday had been fleeting and made in jest, but Craig's doubt about their age difference still lingered.

Caroline was young and adventurous and had her whole life in front of her. And she was full of surprises. Every time Craig found out something new about her, he was taken aback. He shouldn't have been shocked since she'd grown up traveling all over the world and had experienced things most people could only dream about.

He was beginning to think that there was nothing she couldn't do. Last night, he'd learned that she could easily count cards and would hold on to a winning hand before folding so that his competitive grandparents didn't get so huffy at losing. And now, this morning, he was still in a state of wonder at how well she rode a horse.

But looking the part was easy. Real ranch work was tough, and if Craig were to ever change his mind and get married, it would have to be to someone mature, someone who could step up to that kind of responsibility.

"I don't think I've ever seen a more perfect sunrise," Caroline called over her shoulder as they approached the trailhead. A pinkish glow outlined the mountains off in the distance and when he turned to look in that direction, he was immediately reminded of the exact shade of her dusky nipples last night as he'd cupped her breasts in his hands.

Groaning, Craig shoved his Stetson lower on his forehead and asked, "Are you ready to head back now?"

"Back to the ranch? Sure." Caroline clicked her tongue at the mare, then pulled the reins around until Marley was nose to nose with his own mount. "Back to Rust Creek Falls? Not quite yet."

"You mean you want to stay here?" Craig felt the creases on his forehead push against his hat brim.

"I would love that." Her smile was bold and confident. "If I didn't have Josselyn and Drew's wedding to plan or that Presents for Patriots party we're hosting next week, I'd be all for staying right here with you."

"That's because it's the slow season now." Craig squeezed his knees against his stallion's sides to get moving. "Give it a day or two during calving season when we're busy from sunup to sundown rotating the herds, re-seeding our grazing pastures, maintaining the equipment and then spending the entire night on birthing watch. You'll think the chores will never end."

"I don't mind hard work." Caroline shrugged.

"Well, working hard at planning parties and working hard at wrangling cattle during a muddy spring are two different things."

"Says who?" she asked, and he recognized that squared-off shape to her shoulders. "I've never worked on a ranch and I'm guessing that you've never pulled off a successful outdoor wedding for four hundred guests in the middle of a thunderstorm. Therefore, neither one of us would be qualified to make those kinds of comparisons about whose job is more difficult. But if you know someone who has done both, then I'd be glad to hear the results of their findings."

"Fair enough," Craig replied. "There's no way I could do what you do for a living."

"Is that why you were so quick to beat a hasty retreat every time you dropped me off at my office this week?"

"Pretty much." He nodded. "Discussing flower arrangements and table seatings and poofy white dresses surely has to be one of the most headache-inducing tasks on this earth. Just thinking about dealing with all those brides and their talk of having a perfect day makes me squirm."

"Says the man who works with bulls and artificial insemination," she replied.

"Exactly. I *still* wouldn't trade any of my duties on the ranch for any of the mind-boggling demands and events you have to wrestle with every day. Except for maybe cake tasting. I could probably handle that responsibility."

Caroline laughed. "I bet you could handle any responsibility where you're in charge."

"Are you calling me bossy?"

"I'm just saying that you really like to look out for other people."

Craig grunted, unsure whether that was supposed to be a compliment or not, then clicked his tongue at his stallion to move along. "Come on, Jake."

"Jake?" Caroline said, drawing on her own reins to slow down. "You've got to be kidding me."

"What's wrong?" he asked, appraising her startled expression for any sign of injury.

"Let me get this straight. Are we currently riding horses named after Ebenezer Scrooge's business partner—Jacob Marley?"

"Technically my horse's name is Jake, not Jacob. And C.C. named your horse after that book about the dog." Still, Craig couldn't deny the coincidences of so many references to *A Christmas Carol*. But he merely faked a casual shrug and urged his horse forward.

They trotted along silently for a few minutes and then she eased her mount closer to his as the trail narrowed. She really was accommodating nicely to this different style of saddle and it made Craig wonder if she could actually accommodate other parts of his life.

No. He shouldn't even be letting his mind wander in that direction.

"Did you always want to be a wedding

planner?" he asked. Not that he would ever want a woman to give up her career to better facilitate his own. But it wouldn't hurt to confirm that there was no chance she was actually willing to relocate to Thunder Canyon and become a cattle hand. The confirmation would be another red flag to add to his list of warnings on why he shouldn't let their relationship go any further.

"No way." Caroline chuckled. "I didn't know a thing about the industry until Vivienne Shuster hired me."

"So then how did you end up in Rust Creek Falls?"

"I'll tell you if you promise not to laugh at me." Her face was solemn as she held up her palm, as if she was expecting him to repeat an oath. Craig humored her by crossing his finger over his heart. "It's a long story, so I won't go into the boring details, but when I was fifteen, my mom was doing a lecture series at the University of Montana about the history of overlooked female buffalo hunters. Anyway, I fell in love with the area and the campus, breaking my parents' hearts because they'd hoped I'd choose to attend an Ivy League school."

"Why would I laugh at that?" Craig sat up

a little straighter as he surveyed the land. "I definitely can't blame you for loving Montana."

"That's not the odd part. So I visited Rust Creek Falls a couple of years ago before I graduated college. And I... Well, let's just say I had a premonition."

"A premonition?"

"You promised. No laughing." She narrowed her gaze at him until he forced the smirk from his face. Then she continued, "I have a degree in biology. Trust me, I understand science and reason and, therefore, realize exactly how crazy this must all sound. But the truth is, I've always known I had a destiny."

"And planning weddings in Rust Creek Falls is your destiny?" Craig was trying to make sense of it without appearing to sound doubtful.

"Ever since I was a little girl, I've dreamt of getting married. Not like in a creepy Miss-Havisham-pining-for-a-bridegroom sort of way, but just in an excited, purpose-driven way."

"A purpose-driven way?" he repeated. Like she'd been so determined to get married, her brain seized on the first potential groom it could find and then completely fabricated him as the lucky guy? But before he could go down that road, she continued on.

"When I was debating where to move after graduation, I saw an online ad for an assistant wedding planner and it just seemed logical that if I wanted to eventually get married, I should work around like-minded people."

"Like-minded people?"

"Why do you keep repeating everything I say?" she asked and he shrugged. He had no idea why he was having such difficulty wrapping his brain around her words. "Anyway, I saw the job opening as a way to reach my destiny."

"So your destiny is to get married? That's it?"

"Well, to get married to the right man, obviously."

"And how are you supposed to know if you find the right man?"

"I already have." Caroline smiled and Craig's stomach dropped.

"But *how*?"

"Like I said, I can't really explain it. I've always been of the mind-set that I'll know when I know. And finally, I know."

Craig hadn't noticed that his horse was completely standing still as he stared at Caroline. Surely she wasn't saying that she thought *he* was her destiny or that they were meant to be together in some mystical way. He'd promised not to laugh, but he couldn't prevent the sarcasm lacing his voice. "Sounds very scientific."

"Science can explain a lot of things, but it can't always explain emotions. Some intuitions are so powerful, they just feel right. Okay, let me try and break it down another way. Have you ever felt so connected to someone or something that you just knew it was part of your future?"

"This ranch," Craig admitted. "I always knew I was going to work the land and carry on my family's legacy."

He didn't admit that he'd originally planned to do so with Tina.

"So just out of curiosity," she asked as she tilted her head, "if ranching is such grueling work, why do you do it?"

"Because I couldn't imagine doing anything else."

"What about the rodeo?" she asked.

"Life is full of detours, I guess."

"Exactly. Some people might refer to those detours as fate. As though there's a driving force that brings you right to where you belong."

"If by *driving force* you mean a busted collarbone, then yeah, that's what brought me home."

"So that's how you got your scar?" She reached out toward him, but the horses kept them too far apart.

He touched the warm, jagged line along his neck. "Not exactly."

The silence hung between them, but as the wooden outbuildings appeared in the distance she asked, "Then was it another detour?"

Chapter 15

"When I was twenty-one, I was coming home from my engagement party of sorts in Kalispell," Craig began. He continued talking but he'd used his boot heels to urge Jake forward, so he was no longer making eye contact with her as he spoke, and all Caroline could focus on were the three words he'd said. *My engagement party.*

He'd been engaged before. She gave her reins more slack and Marley took the few steps to catch up when she heard him say something about a crash.

"What kind of crash?" she asked, her pulse pounding. "What happened?"

"Tina didn't get to see her cousins very often, so she wanted to go out to a bar with them after the party. I was exhausted and needed to be back in Thunder Canyon early the next morning to meet with the veterinarian about one of our prize heifers. Tina wasn't a drinker and told me that she was fine to drive home while I slept in the passenger seat."

Tina.

Caroline's heart was clawing for more information, needing to know more about the woman Craig had been in love with, but she pressed her lips into a tight line, letting him tell his story uninterrupted.

"The highway patrol officer who did the investigation said she probably didn't even see the stalled logging trailer when she took the turnoff too quickly."

Caroline's hand flew to her mouth. Oh, no. Craig's strange reaction to his parents' not wanting him to drive last night when he was tired suddenly made more sense. It was then that she recalled his tension during the first half of the drive here yesterday and she blurted out, "The cross!"

"What?" Craig's head pivoted toward her as though he'd just remembered she was still beside him, still listening.

"We passed a white wooden cross when we were on Highway 90," Caroline offered.

"That's where her Jeep went off the embankment. She'd swerved, but the left fender still swiped the back of the trailer. The initial collision woke me up, but by then we were already skidding off the road. It was her daddy's old ranch vehicle and the windshield was one of those fold-down types. The hinges had gotten rusty, so when we rolled, the impact caused the whole thing to go in the opposite direction toward us. I don't remember landing, but when I came to, the top corner of the windshield frame had me pinned against the roll bar."

By this time, the horses were standing still again, as though Jake and Marley were in equal stages of grief and couldn't move. Anguish covered Craig's face and Caroline wanted to climb down off the mare and drag him into her embrace. She wanted to hold him, to comfort him. "How long were you stuck like that?"

"The responding officer said it was only five minutes. The driver of the stalled rig had seen us go off the road and called 9-1-1."

"And Tina?" Caroline asked, already knowing the answer.

"We should've driven a safer vehicle, but I'd just sold my truck because we were saving money to build our own house on the property line between our parents' places. The Jeep was built well before anyone had even heard of airbags. Hell, it was so old, we only had lap belts. So there was no way to prevent the steering wheel from breaking her ribs and puncturing her lung."

Caroline bit down hard to force back the gasp rising in her throat, then looked up toward the sky to keep the tears from trickling out of the corners of her eyes.

"I couldn't get to her." Craig's voice was flat when he spoke again. Flat and so defeated. It made the tears Caroline had been holding back spill over. "I fought against the broken windshield but the struggle drove it in deeper. The only part of her I could reach was her hand. I was holding it when she took her last breath and all I could think was that it should have been me driving. I was supposed to protect her. She was looking at me, smiling at me, before she died. But I couldn't save her."

"I can't imagine how painful that must have been for you, Craig. I'm so sorry."

His only acknowledgment of her condolences was a brief nod. "We'd grown up together and had always planned to eventually join our families' cattle operations. But being here at the ranch was a constant reminder of that dream dying alongside her on the highway. I stayed long enough for her funeral, but left for Billings the next day. I had a friend doing the PBR circuit and, at the time, it seemed like traveling from town to town while simultaneously punishing my body in the arena would be the easiest escape."

"But then you came back." Caroline understood why he'd left, yet she also understood why he couldn't stay away. Not only was this land beautiful, but it also filled a person with a sense of peace. A sense of belonging.

"Yep. A few broken bones and one career-ending surgery later, I came home. I had nowhere else. She was gone, but I could still make the ranch live on."

"You must have really loved her," Caroline whispered. He possibly loved her still.

Craig was gazing at something in the horizon, seemingly lost in his own world, when he said, "Tina was the perfect woman for me."

"I think Tina would've loved her," Will said as he drove the all-terrain vehicle along the perimeter of his property the following day.

Craig kept his hat low and his face averted, studying his brother's fence line for any loose posts or fallen wires. "Loved who?"

"Caroline. You know? The woman you're engaged to?"

Clenching his back molars together as Will swerved to avoid a rut in the narrow dirt trail, Craig tried to remember why he'd agreed to come to Will's ranch today and help him do some minor repairs before the breeding season started. Oh, because he'd poured his heart out to Caroline yesterday morning in Thunder Canyon and then she'd barely said a word to him the entire drive home last night.

Her home, that was. Not *his* home. Craig didn't really know what to call the little rental house here in Rust Creek Falls. Although, he'd packed a second duffel bag and brought it with him as if he'd planned to move into the place with her.

It had been late when they'd finally pulled

into her driveway, and while he'd been relieved that she didn't invite him to sleep in her bed with her again, Craig had spent the remainder of the night on the sofa wondering if he'd done something to hurt her feelings.

When an emergency call came in this morning from a bride demanding Caroline drive to some dress shop in Kalispell, Craig grabbed his keys off the hook by the kitchen. But Caroline insisted that she could drive herself and then proceeded to tell him in painful detail what it would be like when an elderly, no-nonsense seamstress told a very vain and very stubborn bride that she would need to lay off all the bridal shower cake and mimosas if she wanted to fit into her dress on her wedding day.

So instead of subjecting himself to that particular brand of misery—which was only slightly worse than worrying about Caroline driving herself—Craig had accepted Will's request for help on his ranch. Too bad they couldn't have taken a good old-fashioned work truck out to the fields instead of this four-wheel-drive Raptor.

"We're not engaged," Craig ground out as his stiff neck rocked side to side against the five-point harness. "Remember, I already told all of you about her head injury and the confabulation and how she thinks I'm her fiancé."

"So then why don't you just explain it to her like you did to all of us? She seems like a smart woman to me." Will looked in his review mirror, probably to make sure one of the shovels hadn't bounced out after that last bump.

"She's incredibly smart. But it doesn't have anything to do with intelligence. Drew said that it's her *brain* tricking her, not me. So no matter what I tell her, she's going to listen to her brain."

"Then what happens when her brain stops tricking her?"

"What do you mean?" Craig snatched his hat off his head because he was tired of adjusting it every time his skull banged into the headrest.

"Well, eventually, she's going to get her memory back. What are you going to do then?"

"I've been trying to figure that out. Jeez, Will, have you ever thought of getting a bulldozer out here and doing a little grading? Perhaps smoothing out a real road?"

"What's there to figure out?" Will asked. "From what I can tell, she's perfect for you. That's why I said that Tina would've loved her."

"Caroline? But she and Tina are nothing alike."

"Apparently, both of them wanted to marry you, which means they were born with the same misguided taste in guys." Before Craig could bark out a retort, Will purposely swerved the ATV to hit a bump in the road, making Craig's butt completely lift off the seat.

"If you keep driving like a maniac, I'm gonna walk back to the stable."

"Speaking of stables, I heard you took Caroline for a ride when you were at Thunder Canyon. Rob said she looked pretty good in the saddle."

"Rob needs to find a woman with her own saddle," Craig muttered.

"Jealous much?" his brother asked, then chuckled.

Craig only growled.

"My point," Will continued and Craig pinched the bridge of his nose since there was apparently no end to this conversation in sight, "is that Caroline seemed pretty comfortable on a horse. Hell, she seemed pretty comfortable in general out there on the ranch. I know that's what you're looking for in a wife."

"I'm not looking for a wife."

"She's also diplomatic and intuitive and has a good head on her shoulders," Will went on as though he hadn't heard Craig's objection. "Plus, I heard you've been eating all of your meals at her house, so I assume she's a decent cook."

"The best." Craig groaned, thinking of the Nutella-filled crepes she'd whipped up that morning. "But don't tell Meemaw."

"Pish," Will scoffed, then took his foot off the accelerator as they came to the end of the fence line. "As if I want her to think I'm taking Grandpac's side about anything right before she goes Christmas shopping."

A series of beeps chimed and Craig immediately reached for his cell phone, his chest filling with worry that something had happened to Caroline. But it wasn't his phone that had rung.

"That's probably Jordyn," Will said, idling the engine and pulling out his cell phone to read his wife's text. "Like everyone else in town, she's curious about what I've found out about you and Caroline."

Craig rolled his eyes.

"Nooooot muuuuuch." Will sounded out the words as he typed a response.

The phone pinged again.

"Jordyn thinks we might have better luck getting you to talk if you have a couple of beers in you."

"Well, you two would have firsthand experience at how alcohol can lower a person's inhibitions," Craig pointed out.

"I'm going to tell Jordyn that you're teasing us about the night we met." Will began typing and Craig tried to grab the phone from his brother when it vibrated again. "She's suggesting we go out tonight and celebrate your engagement."

"You mean my fake engagement?" Craig asked.

"Who cares if it's real or fake? At least you *got* an engagement, unlike me and Jordyn, who accidentally drank some of Homer Gilmore's spiked punch one night and woke up married."

Craig snorted. At least he hadn't gotten himself into a similar predicament. Although, things seemed to have worked out pretty well for Will and Jordyn.

"I'll tell her we should be done with the south pasture around four," his brother said. "We can hit the Ace in the Hole after that."

"Sorry, man," Craig said, not the least bit

sorry. "Caroline has a meeting with the food and beverage director over at the Maverick Manor late this afternoon. So we'll have to take a pass on the celebration that's really an inquisition."

"No problem." Will tapped at his screen for several seconds, then looked up and smiled. "The Maverick Manor has that fancy bar inside the massive lobby. I just told Jordyn we can all head over there after Caroline's meeting."

Craig had texted her about the last-minute get-together with Will and Jordyn. However, Caroline certainly hadn't been expecting an impromptu engagement party of sorts until Jonathan and Dawn showed up, followed by two of the Clifton sisters with their spouses, along with several of the Stricklands.

When she finally realized what was going on, Caroline wanted to come clean then and there about her restored memory. It was one thing to let people be under a mistaken impression. It was quite another to celebrate it.

Unfortunately, before she could say anything, Ben Strickland raised his glass in a toast. Craig shot death looks at his childhood friend, but didn't correct the well-wishers or turn down any of their hearty congratulations.

Her original question, the one she'd pondered the night of that first intense kiss, returned with a cold force.

Why was Craig going along with this?

Now that she knew about Tina and how he'd tried to save her, Caroline could somewhat understand his desire to redeem himself by taking care of Caroline after her concussion. She could even understand how she might indulge an injured woman by allowing her to go on believing whatever she wanted. However, the thing she absolutely couldn't figure out was why Craig wasn't telling his closest friends and family the truth.

Why was he silently drinking to their toasts instead?

There must be a reason why he hadn't already put a stop to all of this—especially if Craig was still in love with another woman.

The only person who could help solve that riddle was Josselyn Weaver. She'd been there when Caroline had hit her head and then again when Caroline had woken up and thought Craig was her fiancé. But Josselyn wasn't here now, and Drew, who'd also been at the hospital part of the time, was never alone long enough for her to ask any meaningful questions.

Questions such as *What's in it for Craig?* and *How far is he willing to go to keep up this pretense?*

The champagne bubbled inside Caroline's tummy and it felt as if corks were popping inside her head. She needed to go somewhere quiet and think this through before people actually began expecting invitations to their wedding.

"Excuse me," she whispered to Craig, who had just clinked beer bottles with his brother Jonathan. "I need to use the ladies' room."

The tight line of his mouth softened with concern and he put the backs of his fingers to her forehead. "Are you feeling okay? Maybe you shouldn't be drinking so soon after your concussion. I told them you probably weren't up for a big night out like this."

"Did you know that everyone was going to be here?" she asked. "That it was going to be like…this?" She'd caught herself from referring to it as an engagement party, because the idea might fill her with too much hope.

"I had a feeling, but I also knew that when my family and friends get an idea in their heads, they're not going to be deterred. It was either this or risk having everyone show up at your office to offer us their congratulations." His arm was draped around her waist as he leaned down to speak in her ear. Suddenly the champagne bubbles weren't the only thing tingling inside her. "But I can take you home if it's too much."

"No, it's fine," she replied, taking another sip before setting down her glass on the polished mahogany bar inside the old log mansion. "I'll be right back."

A few minutes and two enthusiastic congratulatory hugs later, Caroline stared at her reflection in the mirror over the bathroom sink, telling herself it was too risky to keep this pretense up.

She couldn't very well seduce a man who was probably still in love with someone else. Although, during their quiet drive home last night, she'd wondered more than once if he was staying at her house because he genuinely cared for her.

Touching her lips, Caroline remembered the kiss they'd shared in his childhood bedroom. She might be young and inexperienced, but even she knew that wasn't the type of kiss a man gave a woman if he was only feeling protective. The bottom line was that she'd fallen in love with Craig and her underlying instinct that he was the one for her wasn't likely to go away. However, she needed to know that Craig was with her because he actually loved her, not because he was trying to save her.

Unfortunately, she didn't quite know how to do that without telling Craig that her memory had returned. And if she admitted as much, would he consider his hero duties fulfilled and leave her?

A toilet flushed and Caroline quickly turned on the faucet to pretend she was there to wash her hands and not to give herself a strategic pep talk.

"Just the woman I wanted to see," Cecelia Clifton Pritchett said as she came out of a stall. "You're coming to the Presents for Patriots dinner dance next week, right?"

"Oh, um, yes. Our company is actually sponsoring the event and planning it out at Sawmill Station."

"Good. That means Craig will finally be going to a social function. My big brother needs to get out more. I haven't seen him this happy in a long time."

"Really? Because I was just thinking he

seemed pretty uncomfortable out there with everyone congratulating us on the *engagement*." Caroline emphasized the last word to gauge Craig's sister's reaction.

With the exception of his grandparents, nobody had mentioned their relationship status at Thanksgiving, let alone questioned it. Surely his family must be wondering what was actually going on.

"Nah." Cecelia dried her hands on a paper towel. "He just hates being the center of attention. And, because he carries the world on his shoulders, he probably thinks he should be feeling guilty."

"Guilty?" Caroline's fingers shot up to the V-shaped collar on her dress and toyed with the ruffled edges. "Why would he feel guilty?"

"For finally moving on and allowing himself to open up to someone a second time."

Cecelia stood beside her, applying lipstick while Caroline sucked in her cheeks, fighting the impulse to ask for some sort of proof that Craig really was in fact ready to fall in love again.

Chapter 16

Yesterday, when Will had railroaded him into the party at the Maverick Manor, Craig had known he should level with all of his family and friends. But then the toasts had started and Caroline, who hadn't spoken to him much during their drive home from Thunder Canyon on Friday, had gotten all flushed and became even more subdued before rushing off to the bathroom. He'd been worried that the impromptu celebration was too much for her—especially on the heels of meeting all of his family at Thanksgiving—and he'd just wanted to get her home and comfortable and away from all the pretending.

Other than the accident investigators, Craig had never really spoken to anyone else about the night Tina had died, and maybe he'd been a little too open with Caroline during their ride. But she'd been talking about all that destiny stuff and people knowing where they belong and he needed to make her see that his entire life was the ranch.

That was *his* destiny.

Tina had understood more than anyone else what sacrifices it would take for that lifestyle. But she was gone and Craig would be better off alone than forcing a young and vibrant woman like Caroline into a world that wasn't for her.

It would be one thing if she had her memory back and was able to make rational decisions based on full disclosure. However, he worried that she was just acting upon some childish fantasy of getting married and, as much as he desired her physically, there was no way Craig could be with any woman under false pretenses.

"Let's go get a tree today," Caroline had said that morning, taking a tray of homemade cinnamon rolls out of the oven. "It's going to be a crazy week at work for me and I don't know when I'll have another chance since I've got weddings and parties booked every weekend this month. Besides, Christmas is my absolute favorite holiday and I can't wait to decorate."

Apparently, neither could the rest of Rust Creek Falls, Craig thought grudgingly a couple of hours later when they arrived at the tree lot adjacent to the Masonic Lodge downtown. The town was already getting into the Christmas spirit with lights and garlands going up on Main Street and notices announcing collection locations for Presents for Patriots, as well as the upcoming holiday pageants at the local schools.

"Where are we going to put it?" Craig scratched the back of his neck as he studied the eight-foot-tall Douglas fir.

"If we move one of the bookshelves over to the left, we can put it in front of the living room window."

The word *we* was getting passed around in this conversation an awful lot. But Caroline's eyes were bright and the tip of her nose was turning pink as the first flurries of snowfall dusted the green branches around them. Her enthusiasm for the holidays was contagious, and since the moment she'd opened her eyes in that hospital emergency room, Craig really hadn't been able to deny her anything.

The Freemasons had partnered with the varsity football team to sell Christmas trees as a fund-raiser, and Craig tipped the defensive tackle who'd carried the freshly trimmed bundle to his truck for them.

"Thank you, sir," the teenager said before turning to Caroline, who, in her knit beanie and oversize red plaid scarf, appeared young enough to be the kid's homecoming date. "I'm also supposed to tell all the customers that if you're looking for homemade ornaments or decorations, they're having a craft fair right now inside the high school gym."

Caroline slapped her mitten-covered hands together and gave an excited bounce before turning those pleading, doe-shaped eyes at Craig. And that was how he ended up spending the rest of his Sunday afternoon picking out glass balls covered in glitter, rolling his eyes in camaraderie with the other men hiding out at the hot chocolate stand and tipping his hat at the ladies from the quilting club who offered to sell him a hand-sewn tote bag for all the purchases he was carrying as he walked behind his pretend fiancée.

Not wanting to be a complete Scrooge and begrudge her the excitement and wonder of the season, Craig followed along and whipped out his wallet to pay for her decorations. In fact, if was being honest with himself, he was kind of getting a kick out of her enthusiasm as she practically skipped along, gushing at the displays at each booth.

Later that night, as a cinnamon-scented candle filled the air, they were hanging their new ornaments on the tree that barely fitted inside her tiny house. Caroline reached into one of the paper bags and pulled out matching red velvet stockings with each of their names stitched along the tops.

Craig gulped and all the pleasure from his earlier indulgences faded away, leaving nothing but a guilty taste in his mouth. "When did you get those?"

"I saw them when you were at the caramel corn stand, getting us those popcorn balls. The Embroidery Club was selling them and offered free customizing while we shopped."

"Don't you think we're a little too old for

stockings?" he asked. And where would she even hang the things? It wasn't like she had an actual fireplace in this dollhouse of hers.

"Says the man who ate an entire roll of cherry Life Savers on the drive home." She winked at him. "Didn't you have a stocking growing up?"

"Yeah, but as I got older, my parents put me in charge of filling them for the younger ones. Same thing with hiding the Easter eggs."

"Well, I figured we could start our own family traditions." Her last two words hit him with a force, and panic clawed at the back of his throat.

Or maybe it was guilt. After all, if it wasn't for him going along with all of this imagined-fiancé business, she wouldn't be under the misguided impression that they had any family traditions to start.

Either way, he could feel a line of perspiration dampen his hairline as he studied their embroidered names. The only thing more permanent would've been a tattoo. Or a scar.

He swiped at the prickling skin along his neck.

How could he convince Caroline that she shouldn't allow herself to get too attached to him? That she shouldn't believe this fanciful notion of hers that he was the man for her. If he had permission from Dr. Robinson, he would gladly steer her in that direction right this second.

But since he couldn't risk stressing her out by saying what he wanted, Craig said the first thing he could think of. "There comes a certain point in everyone's life when they need to grow up and stop believing in Santa Claus."

Last night, Caroline had tried to pretend Craig's words hadn't hurt, pasting on her smile that she used when dealing with an overpriced vendor or a client's negative mother-in-law. They'd gotten the Christmas decorations up—minus the stockings, which she'd discreetly slipped back in the bag—and then she'd made creamy tomato basil soup and grilled cheese sandwiches for dinner because that wasn't quite as juvenile as chicken nuggets and tater tots, which were the only things she had in her freezer.

Despite going to bed early to escape the awkward tension, she'd been awake until midnight, tossing and turning and rethinking what he'd said about her believing in childish things. Thank goodness he didn't know about the psychic or he'd really think Caroline was naive and impressionable.

If she and Craig were meant to be together, then Caroline needed to prove to him once and for all how much of a woman she was.

Sitting at the conference table in her office that morning, Caroline stared absently at her blank notepad, trying to figure out how to do that. Cecelia had implied that Craig was willing to move on, so maybe it wouldn't be such a bad thing for Caroline to seduce him after all.

She tapped her pencil against her chin. The problem with that was she didn't know how to go about it. Especially since her past attempts at physical intimacy with Craig had been rather unsuccessful and only left her wanting more.

"I go away for two weeks and come back to find my favorite employee engaged."

At the sound of the familiar voice, Caroline looked up to see Vivienne entering the office.

Smiling widely and looking sun-kissed and refreshed from her honeymoon in Fiji, she gushed, "I can't wait to hear all about it."

"Yeah, it kinda happened fast," Caroline

said, then let out a deep breath and slouched against the chair's brightly upholstered fabric. "The engagement, that is. It took on a life of its own, if that makes any sense."

"You have no idea how much sense that makes to me." Vivienne gave a little chuckle. "Did I ever tell you how Cole made up an entire fiancée in order to have me plan his pretend wedding?"

"But Cole loves you," Caroline said, referring to Vivienne's new husband.

"He barely knew me when he came up with the plan."

"What plan?" Josselyn Weaver asked as she came into the office for her rescheduled consultation. Ever since their first meeting had ended in a hospital stay, Caroline had the feeling her client had been purposely avoiding her. Fortunately, the woman still had a wedding to plan, which meant Caroline could finally get some answers.

"We were just talking about my engagement." Caroline studied her for any signs of conspiracy. Josselyn gave a discreet cough and looked away, practically inviting the next question. "Did you know I wasn't engaged to Craig when I woke up in that hospital?"

Josselyn gasped before narrowing her eyes. "Wait. Did *you* know you weren't engaged to him?"

"Not at the time I didn't." Caroline sighed in frustration, sinking lower in her seat. "I really believed he was my fiancé when I first saw him."

"But now you know…" Josselyn made a circular motion with her wrist, encouraging Caroline to fill in the blanks. "What exactly do you know?"

Caroline went on to tell the two women about everything, from Winona Cobbs to her late-night research on confabulation to how her memory had come back as soon as Craig kissed her.

"So you guys kissed?" Josselyn asked, settling down into one of the chairs at the conference table. "How was that?"

"Wonderful and confusing and then wonderful again when I met his family."

"Oh, boy, you already met his family?" Vivienne asked, joining them at the table.

"Yes. I went there for Thanksgiving. And then some of them and his friends had this impromptu engagement party for us at the Maverick Manor the other night and everyone was congratulating us, and I sat there, knowing the truth yet saying nothing."

"Well," Josselyn started, "if it's any consolation, Craig also knew you weren't really engaged."

"Exactly. Craig knew it and, for the life of me, I can't figure out why he would go along with a pretend engagement." Caroline placed her elbow on the table and braced her forehead in her hand. "Who else knows it isn't real?"

"Well, Drew and I knew since we were there at the hospital when you came to and made the surprising announcement. Sorry for not speaking up sooner about that, by the way. The doctor didn't want us saying anything that could give you any more anxiety. Plus, Drew promised me that you were in good hands with Craig."

"But what does his family think of your relationship?" Vivienne asked.

"I'm not sure what they think." Caroline looked over to Josselyn, who only smirked.

"So, I wasn't able to attend the party at the Maverick Manor, but I heard that his siblings nominated Cecelia to be the one to tell you that they approved of the engagement."

Her tummy flipped in excitement. Having the rest of the Clifton family's approval boosted her confidence. But just to be sure her feelings weren't completely one-sided, she asked, "You guys don't think all of this is totally nuts?"

"From what I understand, there have been crazier courtships in Rust Creek Falls," Vivienne offered. "If you want him, I say go after him."

"I definitely want him, but only if he wants me in return. What happens, though, when he realizes that I remember everything? Will he be relieved that he can finally walk away?" Caroline rested her head against the back of the chair and studied the ceiling. "How do I come clean and still keep my cowboy?"

"I don't know Craig as well as the rest of the Stricklands do." Josselyn leaned forward and wiggled her eyebrows. "But I've seen the way that man looks at you."

Hope blossomed in Caroline's chest and she sat up straighter. "How does he look at me?"

"Like he's in no hurry to walk away."

She sincerely hoped that Josselyn was right. But just to be sure, Caroline decided to take matters into her own hands.

Chapter 17

"Your drink matches your outfit," Craig said over the strains of the band's rendition of Mariah Carey's "All I Want for Christmas."

"Huh?" Caroline's nerve endings were pulsating along with the tempo of the festive music.

He nodded at her rum-laced eggnog in a miniature Mason jar and repeated himself.

Caroline had carefully chosen an ivory cashmere sweater and paired it with a matching fitted skirt that flared into a short ruffle of chiffon above the knee. Despite the snow outside, she'd kept her legs bare and her feet festive in a pair of glittery gold pumps. "Well, that's a party planner's job. To work from behind the scenes and blend in with the surroundings."

"As if you could ever blend in anywhere," Craig said, his unconcealed stare turning her pulsing nerves into a throbbing ache under her skin.

It was the night of the Presents for Patriots fund-raiser and they hadn't driven to the party together because, technically, Caroline was working. At least she had been the first half of the evening. But the caterers and the band and even the bartenders had worked previous events at Sawmill Station and didn't need much direction. So, after dinner and the silent auction, the only thing left for her to do was dance.

Of course, the sexy cowboy standing in front of her didn't seem all that eager to pull her onto the dance floor despite the fact that his warm hands kept sliding lower along her back each time he'd come over to check on how she was feeling.

In fact, judging by the way his palm was now resting along the upper curve of her bottom and threatening to dip lower, Caroline got the impression that he was much more eager to get her alone.

And truthfully, Caroline didn't want to wait any longer to make Craig hers.

They'd been living together for almost two weeks now and there was no way she was going to let him sleep on her sofa one more night. Maybe it was the intoxicating fragrance of all the swags of pine branches and mistletoe running along the white linen-covered farm tables. Or maybe it was the warm glow from the white twinkling lights hanging from the rustic wooden beams of the old freight house. Perhaps it was the spiced eggnog concoction warming her veins. More than likely, it was a combination of all three making her grow bolder and more confident by the minute.

It was either now or never.

"Are you ready to go home?" she asked, turning toward him and laying her hand on the lapel of his dark sport coat. "I want to give you your Christmas present early."

She saw the muscles of his neck contract as he tipped back his head and swallowed down the rest of his beer. Setting his empty bottle on the nearest table, his voice was low and rushed when he said, "Let's go."

Vivienne—who was standing with her husband beside the vintage red sleigh loaded with gifts donated for the Presents for Patriots charity—gave Caroline a thumbs-up as Craig guided her toward the exit.

The ten-minute ride back to her house was the same one he drove every day. But now it seemed as though it only took seconds before they were pulling into Caroline's driveway.

Maybe he knew what she had planned and he was just as eager for it. Snow was falling as they walked to her front door, yet her skin was on fire and anticipation raced through her. The sight of her spare key attached to his key ring gave her another jolt of confidence that Craig wasn't in a hurry to go anywhere. At least, not yet.

"Wait here," she said, pointing toward the sofa because it would've been too mortifying to suggest he wait on her bed. And trickier to explain without giving the surprise away. And she had a feeling that she was going to need the element of surprise.

Caroline went into her bathroom and carefully removed her sweater and skirt, then reached in the vanity to find the matching lace bra-and-pantie set she'd hidden there for this exact moment.

Her cheeks turned the same crimson shade as the lingerie and Caroline was glad she'd been smart enough not to wear such a sexy thing under her clothes earlier. She would've been entirely distracted throughout the party, constantly aware of what she had on underneath and thinking about who would see it later.

She was dying to splash some cold water on her face, but didn't want to ruin her carefully applied makeup. Instead, she settled for a gulp of water out of the faucet, then stared at her reflection wondering if there was anything she'd forgotten when she'd come up with this plan. *Don't think of it as a plan*, she told herself. *Try to act natural.*

Unfortunately, the longer she stood in this bathroom, the more she would second-guess herself. Steeling herself, she listened to that initial instinct—the one that had never steered her wrong before—and walked out into the living room.

Caroline heard Craig's sharp intake of breath, saw the heat fill his eyes, and it was all she could do not to smile in triumph. She was sure he could see her heart thumping behind her rib cage.

"I have to tell you something," Craig blurted out. His voice held a slight tremble and Caroline guessed that he was just as nervous as she. Another ounce of courage filled her and she straightened her back, causing her breasts to thrust forward.

"Don't you want to unwrap your gift first?" she asked.

His only response was his Adam's apple bobbing up and down. Normally, when he was uncomfortable or trying to avoid a question, he focused on some distant point while he spoke to her. Right now, though, his eyes were drilling into her, and Caroline's confidence soared.

He'd already discarded both his heavier outer coat and his sport coat and was now only wearing a white dress shirt. She walked toward him and slid her hands up his chest until her fingers landed on the first buttonhole. "Or can I unwrap mine first?" she asked him as she opened his buttons.

"I'm not who you think I am," he said in a rush, and Caroline didn't quite feel like herself, either. Boldness had overcome her, and right now, if she allowed him to distract her with all his chivalrous excuses of why they couldn't be intimate, she would surely lose more than her memory. She might lose her mind.

Putting a finger up to his mouth to gently shush him, Caroline ended up tracing his lower lip. "But you're exactly who I want."

"How do you *know*, though? Your head—"

She cut off his words with a kiss. Caroline was tired of explaining that her concussion was perfectly healed. Her only option now was to show him. And she did so with her mouth, her hands, her entire body, distracting him from any argument about why they shouldn't finally consummate their relationship.

There was a slight resistance when she tugged on his hand, trying to lead him toward her bedroom, and she could see all the conflicted emotions pass across his face. Cupping his cheek, she whispered, "Craig, trust me, I know what you want to tell me. But there isn't a single thing you can say that would stop me from wanting you. Unless it's that you don't want me."

"Nothing could be further from the truth,"

he replied, his voice deep and loaded with desire.

"Then prove it."

Craig groaned as he lifted her into his arms and carried her the rest of the way to the bed. His mouth claimed hers and as he set her down, she slipped her hands into his undone shirt and yanked it free just as his body followed hers onto the comforter.

There was more kissing, more touching, more moaning as her bra came loose and her panties slid from her hips. Caroline was pushing his jeans past the rounded muscles of his rear end when his body stilled.

"I need to go get some protection," he murmured against her temple, then began to push off her, but she wrapped her legs around his waist and pulled him back.

"Don't leave," Caroline said, thinking she would die of humiliation if he came to his senses and rejected her now.

"Honey, I'm just going to the living room to get them out of my duffel bag."

Pleasure engulfed her as she realized that he must have known in the back of his mind that they would eventually make love. He'd prepared just as she had.

"That's okay," she replied, leaning toward her bedside drawer to retrieve the package she'd brought home from work. "I was too embarrassed to go to the drugstore in town, so I found these in one of the favor bags we had left over from a bachelorette party last summer."

When he rolled the condom on, Caroline knew with a certainty that this was the man for her. This was her destiny. He entered her slowly and Caroline gasped as the hard tip filled her.

"Are you okay?" he asked and she could hear the tension in his tone, as it must've taken him an extreme amount of willpower to hold himself back.

"I've never been better," she sighed. "Please don't stop now."

"I never can tell you no," Craig said, then thrust deep inside her, only to freeze when she winced in pain. "You…you're a…"

"I'm yours," Caroline said, using her calves to wind around him and draw him in closer.

She'd been a virgin, Craig thought, trailing his fingers along her spine as she curved her body next to his afterward. There was no turning back now. Caroline had unwittingly given him a precious gift and all he'd given her in return was false hope.

Unless…

What would happen if Caroline never regained her memory and went on believing they were engaged? Could Craig actually go through with their marriage? The past couple of weeks, he hadn't faked his attraction for her or even how much he cared about her. In fact, the more he'd gotten to know her, the more he could see that she was well educated and determined to live her life the way she wanted.

And apparently, she wanted him.

Caroline sighed and hooked her left leg over his thigh. His own arm under her shoulders instinctively pulled her closer, as though he could never get enough of her. And deep down, he knew that would be the case. How could he possibly let her go now?

If she really wanted that life to be on the ranch in Thunder Canyon, there was no way he would be able to tell her no. Besides, Craig was tired of being the voice of reason.

The truth of the matter was that the night she'd pulled out those matching Christmas stockings, he'd been terrified at first. But as he'd battled sleep all night on her sofa, he'd come to the conclusion that he could no longer imagine his life without Caroline in it. All he could hope was that, if she remembered nothing else, she knew that he'd always tried to do the right thing.

Her left hand was absently caressing his chest and Craig knew that if she continued, he would want her on her back again. Or on top of him this time. As great as their first time had felt, he didn't want to make her sore—or at least sorer than he'd probably already made her. Using his palm, he cupped her hand in his, slowing her motion.

After a couple of seconds, he found himself stroking her left ring finger, the one that had remained bare throughout all of this supposed engagement. Craig froze at the realization, wondering how both of them had overlooked something so obvious.

"Are you okay?" Caroline propped her chin up on her right hand. Her brown hair was thoroughly disheveled and hanging in messy waves around her face and she had never looked more adorable or more loved.

Oh, God. He'd fallen in love with her.

The realization should have made him go cold and sink into the bed with fear of the unexpected. Instead, Craig basked in the warmth of Caroline's heated body as a feeling of weightlessness and euphoria settled into a cocoon around him.

"Actually," he said, unable to stop the smile that played on his lips as he began tracing her ring finger again, "I was just thinking we should go to a jeweler to pick something out soon."

Caroline gasped before scrambling up to her knees, not bothering to take the bedsheet with her as she beamed a smile at him. "You mean an engagement ring?"

"Of course," Craig said, then chuckled as she rained kisses down over his face.

"I—" she kissed his cheek "—love—" she kissed his forehead "—you—" she kissed his chin "—so—" she kissed his other cheek "—much." She kissed his lips. Then she held her face over his and he saw the depth of her happiness reflected in her eyes. "I was hoping that you'd propose by Christmas."

Hearing her say that she loved him gave Craig the strength to take over the world. Or at least to flip her over and take his time covering her with kisses.

But then he heard her last sentence.

"Propose?" He braced his hands against her shoulders, holding her in place and preventing her from distracting him anymore with her full, sensuous lips. "But we're already engaged."

"Not officially, though."

"What do you mean 'not officially'?"

"Craig." Caroline opened and closed her mouth several times. "Look, I know you were a good sport to go along with all those things I said after I bumped my head. I can't imagine how crazy you must've thought I was. But we can stop all the pretending now, can't we?"

"Hold on." Something clawed at his throat and it took several attempts to swallow the shock down. "You got your memory back?"

Chapter 18

"Technically, I've always had my memory." Caroline's smile was less dreamy this time and a bit more sheepish, and the hair on the back of Craig's neck stood at attention. "I just also had one additional memory that wasn't quite real."

"When did you realize we weren't engaged?" He had a million questions he wanted to ask, but that sensation that had clawed at his neck earlier was now throbbing near his ears and he wasn't sure he wanted to hear the answers.

Caroline sat up much less playfully than

she had earlier and slowly tucked the bedsheet under her arms. "The first night you kissed me. I knew there was no way I could've forgotten something like that. Everything came flooding back."

"You mean, you knew for almost two weeks and never told me the truth?"

"I thought…" Her voice trailed off and two little creases appeared above her nose.

"No. Don't give me that confused, hopeless, please-rescue-me face," Craig said and could see by her recoil that his words had hit their mark. He stood up and snatched his jeans off the floor before continuing, "I'm the one who should be confused. I'm the one who looks like the hopeless fool. I'm the one who got played."

He heard her indrawn breath before he'd scooped up his abandoned dress shirt, shoving his arms through the sleeves as he stomped out of the bedroom. In the living room, he fumbled with his boots, anger blinding him and frustration making his motions erratic. He needed to get out of this house. He needed to get away from Caroline, away from all the deception.

It felt good to slam the front door behind

him, until he realized that he'd forgotten his keys in the pocket of his winter coat. The coat he'd left inside, along with his hat and his dignity.

But there was no way he'd go back inside to retrieve his belongings. At least not now. He stared at his truck covered with at least two inches of snow, shivering when he realized the crew cab doors were locked and he couldn't climb inside for warmth. All he had on was jeans, a thin dress shirt and boots, minus the socks. He wasn't sure where those had ended up earlier in the evening when he'd been in a blinded hurry to shed his clothes and feel Caroline's skin pressed against his.

Crunching the fresh powdery snow under his heels, Craig strode toward the street, refusing to think about the cold or about Caroline's warm naked body. His heartbeat pounded in time to each angry step he took. He should call someone for a ride, but he'd been so stupid in his rage, he'd also forgotten his phone and his wallet.

Had he ever been this upset before?

With no destination in mind, he thought about continuing down to the boardinghouse to get a room for the night, but Melba and

Gene Strickland were pretty old-fashioned when it came to relationships and the types of people they allowed to stay at their place. They likely preferred a guest who didn't show up and disturb them in the middle of the night after a reckless bout of lovemaking with a woman who'd been pretending to be his fiancée.

Instead, Craig made a left at the corner and found himself walking down Rust Creek Falls's picture-perfect Main Street. As a kid, he'd remembered a pay phone in front of Crawford's General Store, but when he arrived, he saw that it was long gone. Just like his youth. Just like his common sense.

Caroline probably didn't even know what a pay phone was, Craig thought as he kicked through the layer of snow on the sidewalk. He should've known better than to fall under the young woman's spell. His life had been exactly the way he'd wanted it before he walked into that wedding planner's office. Before he'd rushed to save a pretty stranger from knocking herself out. Before it was *his* world that got knocked off its axis.

The twinkling Christmas lights along Main Street mocked him, each blink reminding

Craig of the holiday he didn't know he'd been looking forward to. The holiday he'd been starting to think of as his and Caroline's.

They were going to do the Candlelight Walk together and he'd envisioned the two of them wrapping presents side by side at the community center next week for Presents for Patriots. He'd even planned to take her home to Thunder Canyon and hang their matching stockings over the family's huge fireplace on Christmas Eve. The stockings he'd made fun of.

The life he'd thought he no longer wanted.

Originally, he'd wanted a partner for the ranch. A helpmate. Now, though, all he wanted was her.

His brain told him that there could be no love if there wasn't trust. Yet, at the same time, his heart told him that there could be no love if he wasn't with Caroline.

Craig's steps slowed and, as his anger cooled, so did the rest of his body. Shoving his hands into his front pockets, he arched his back, bracing against the cold wind pummeling him from behind.

"Craig!"

He whipped around to see Caroline rushing toward him, balancing a bundle in front of her as she navigated the icy sidewalk in faded jeans and cowboy boots. Bright turquoise ones and, judging by the worn leather, not exactly new. So she *did* own a pair after all.

He tried to tell himself that it didn't mean anything. It didn't mean that she belonged on his ranch or in his world. But then he saw what she was carrying and his breath left his body, his ribs squeezing against his lungs.

"When I noticed that you didn't take your truck, I was worried about you being outside in this weather without your coat." Caroline handed him the folded sheepskin coat with his Stetson hat on top, then, without saying another word, she turned around and walked back toward Cedar Street. She didn't apologize or make excuses or try to convince him to come back to her house to talk things out.

Was she really just going to let him go?

Craig slammed the hat onto his head and began walking after her, tempted to ask about his truck keys. As he was shrugging on his jacket, something fell to the ground. He reached down and came back up with a wool scarf. This wasn't his. When had he ever worn a scarf?

Yet the sight of the red plaid pattern stopped him in his tracks. Her scarf.

She'd chased after him. On foot and in the middle of the night with snow barreling down on her, Caroline had trekked along the frozen sidewalks just to bring him a damn scarf. She'd given him her trust. She'd given him her virginity. She'd given him her love.

And he didn't even have the decency to say thank you.

Now it was his turn to chase after her.

"Caroline, wait," Craig called out as he quickly caught up with her at the corner. She didn't turn around, but at least she stopped. "Thank you for bringing my coat."

He saw the back of her head nod and his stomach clenched. She took another step and Craig suddenly didn't want her to leave.

"How did you know where I would go?" he asked, burying his hands in his fur-lined pockets and rocking back on his heels. His bare feet slipped inside his boots and he cursed himself for forgetting his socks.

Caroline turned around and, in the dim glow of the old-fashioned streetlamp, he could see the dark sadness in her usually bright eyes. "I followed the footprints. Apparently, you're the only fool running around downtown Rust Creek Falls in the middle of a snowstorm."

"I definitely feel like a fool," Craig admitted.

"And you don't think I felt like a fool, too?" Caroline's face tilted up and he could see that the normally happy and composed wedding planner was also willing to fight some battles.

Originally, Caroline was only going to make sure Craig wasn't wandering the streets of Rust Creek Falls without a coat, his stubbornness exposing him to the bone-chilling elements. She'd anticipated him being annoyed that she hadn't told him about her memory returning earlier and she didn't blame him for that. However, she wasn't the only person who'd done some misleading in this relationship. In fact, if anyone had been played the fool, it had been her.

"*I* was the one who looked like an idiot when I fell off a stupid chair in front of a stranger and hit my head on the ground," Caroline started, the stiffness in her spine having nothing to do with the snowfall or the chill in the air.

"Just for the record," he said, shrugging as if the weather wasn't bothering him at all, "you hit your head on the bookshelf. I caught you before you actually hit the ground."

"Like that makes it any less embarrassing?" Caroline rolled her eyes before continuing. "*I* was the one who woke up in the hospital thinking I was engaged to that same stranger. *I* was the one who insisted you were my fiancé to the doctor, to Josselyn, to everyone who came into my office later that week, despite the fact that I knew all of you were keeping a secret from me. My mother, a national icon for women's rights who doesn't believe in marriage? Yeah, *I* told her we were engaged, while you stood there looking all sexy and shirtless in my kitchen. *I* gushed about our relationship that *you* knew was completely fabricated."

"You thought I looked sexy when I was shirtless?" Craig dipped his chin, lowering his voice.

But Caroline would not be swayed by her body's traitorous reaction to him when she still had things to say. "Yes, I got my memory back that night you first kissed me and didn't tell you. It was selfish of me to keep quiet this past week. But I did it because I fell in love with you and wanted to keep you."

"You wanted to keep me?"

"Of course I did. Craig, I wanted you from that moment you carried the donut box into my office. I never would have believed that we were supposed to be together or said any of those things if I didn't already know in my heart that I meant it. I meant every word I ever said. My feelings for you were never a lie. So, now, tell me your excuse."

"My excuse?"

"Why didn't you tell me the truth from the beginning?"

"Because the doctors told us not to upset you. They said you would eventually remember things at your own pace."

"But you *stayed* at my house. You willingly jeopardized my reputation."

"Dr. Robinson said they couldn't release you from the hospital unless someone could watch out for you. And you were the one insisting I stay with you when Josselyn invited you to recuperate at Sunshine Farm."

"But Dr. Robinson didn't say you had to take me to Thanksgiving dinner with your family." Caroline put her hands on her hips.

"Dr. Robinson didn't say you had to go along with that engagement party at the Maverick Manor."

"Fine. Dr. Robinson didn't say that I had to like being around you either, but guess what? I did. I liked the way you were always positive and happy and made these wonderful home-cooked meals without any vegetables. I liked that you were patient with my bickering grandparents and that you were kind to my grouchy cat and that you slipped a roll of cherry Life Savers into my shirt pocket every afternoon when I picked you up from work. I liked that you knew so many random things about so many subjects and could count cards to come up with the best hand, but were still humble enough to fold and let Meemaw and Grandpac win the game."

Caroline shivered, not from the cold, but from his words. Craig unfolded the red plaid scarf, which was still in his hands, and coiled it around her neck, using the ends to pull her closer to him. "I liked being your fiancé because I like you."

"Just 'like'?" she prompted, walking her fingers up the lapels of his coat as she arched one eyebrow.

"Maybe a little more." Craig groaned when she pulled her hands away from his shoulders. "Okay, a whole lot more. But it took me a full two weeks to fall in love with you. How did you know so soon that I was the one? Would any cowboy who had walked into your office that day have been the man you wanted?"

Caroline's heart fluttered at his words that he'd fallen in love with her. "Have you ever heard of Winona Cobbs?"

"The old psychic?"

Caroline nodded. "Well, she predicted I'd be engaged by Christmas and then she gave me a few clues as to who it would be. The second you walked into my office, I was sure it had to be you. It was my last thought before I hit my head."

"I'll admit, there was something about you in the beginning that made me want to take care of you. I don't know if I agree with all that premonition and destiny stuff, but it's hard to deny that I was in the right place at the right time."

"Or maybe *I* was in the right place at the right time?" Caroline offered. "Maybe *you* were the one who needed rescuing?"

"Only time will tell." Craig smiled, cupping her cheek.

"Then why don't we start over from the beginning and take things slowly?" Caroline stuck out her hand and said, "Hi. My name is Caroline Ruth. It's nice to meet you."

"Hi, Caroline. I'm Craig Clifton and I am completely in love with you." He pulled her hand up to his lips and giddiness bubbled in the back of Caroline's throat. "That should be all the time we need."

As his mouth landed on hers, all either one of them could think was...

Engaged by Christmas.

Epilogue

On Christmas Eve, Craig shifted in his metal folding chair beside Caroline as they watched the elementary school's performance of *A Christmas Carol* at the community center in Thunder Canyon.

"What'd Bob Cratchit say?" Meemaw whispered loudly down their row. She'd had to lean across Grandpac to ask Caroline since Craig's grandfather had been the first to arrive this evening and had used name-badge stickers to save seats for the entire family.

"Dammit, woman," Grandpac whispered back. "Get your hearing aid fixed. And you can't just move your chair and sit wherever you want. You're blocking the aisle."

"Well, seeing as how you conveniently saved my seat on the opposite end of the auditorium, I didn't really have a choice."

"I should've saved a seat for you in the dang parking lot," his grandfather muttered loud enough to draw the attention of the fifth-grade usher.

Craig rolled his eyes, hoping his grandparents didn't completely ruin the surprise he had planned for Caroline. Or worse, get them kicked out of Caroline's favorite holiday play.

"Cratchit is basically telling his wife that it's Christmas and she needs to set a good example for the children by toasting his horrible boss, Mr. Scrooge," Dr. Ruth whispered as he turned around from the row in front of them. Caroline's dad, who'd flown in with Caroline's mom from India late last night, held up the bright screen of his electronic tablet. "I have both the book, as well as the adapted script for the play, loaded on my iPad if you want to follow along."

"Did you know that Charles Dickens never even gave Mrs. Cratchit a first name in the original version?" Dr. Rodriguez put her arm along the back of Caroline's father's seat as she spoke to the entire row behind her. "Because women apparently didn't deserve any sort of notability or recognition in Victorian England."

While Craig had been excited to meet Caroline's parents for the first time, he was also now questioning his own parents' offer to extend an invitation for everyone to come to Thunder Canyon for the holidays. He shifted in his seat again, wishing he had brought Caroline here tonight alone.

"If you ask me, Mrs. Cratchit should tell ol' Bob to shove his brownnosing toast to Scrooge up his—"

"Shhh, Meemaw." Craig pointed to something going on offstage. "The important part is coming up."

The boy who was playing the role of Tiny Tim limped off the stage, trying to hold on to a wrapped gift box that was meowing as the rest of the audience murmured and giggled.

Dr. Ruth held his tablet closer to his face. "I don't remember this happening in the original."

Craig caught the young actor's eye and was about to lift his arm behind Caroline's back to point her out. But Grandpac beat him to it. "She's right here, kiddo. Next to me."

When the little boy set the squirming box on Caroline's lap, he announced in a proud voice, "A Merry Christmas to us all. God bless us everyone!"

The crowd hushed as they swiveled to watch Caroline remove the lid to her gift. Tiny Tim, the feline version, was inside, squatting on his two good hind legs and proudly meowing his normally grouchy head off.

Caroline giggled and lifted the cat out and Rob spoke up from behind Craig's shoulder, "I can't believe you put your poor cat in a box, Craig."

"It was my idea," C.C. said from where she was now standing next to the young actor in the aisle. "And look, Tiny Tim is loving being the center of attention."

The animal was in fact now purring in Caroline's arms, his tail slowly swishing back and forth as if he was ready for his encore. Craig's father hovered behind them, his video camera zooming in.

"Sit down, dear." His mother pushed his father's arm. "I can't see."

"I'm in the middle of something here,"

Craig reminded everyone and Caroline gasped when she saw him drop to his knee.

"Caroline Ruth," he started, and Dr. Rodriguez gave a not-so-discreet cough. "I mean, Caroline Rodriguez Ruth, would you do me the honor of becoming my wife?"

Tiny Tim let out another meow as Craig untied the ribbon attached to his collar and pulled the diamond ring free. "As well as my spoiled cat's adopted mom?"

A tear trickled out of Caroline's eye as she eagerly bobbed her head up and down while Craig slid the ring onto her finger. When he pulled her and Tiny Tim into his arms, the entire community center erupted in applause.

Two months later, Craig was knee-deep in overseeing the cattle breeding season, while Caroline was busy establishing the Thunder Canyon location for her and Vivienne's newest wedding planning office.

But both of them always made time to meet with the architect and builder they'd hired to create their dream home on the Clifton family ranch. There would be a small guest cottage for when Caroline's parents came to town—or for when Grandpac needed a space to cool off after having a big fight with Meemaw during holiday dinners—and there would be plenty of bookshelves for their memories and pillows for Tiny Tim.

Caroline and Craig still hadn't set a wedding date, but now that they'd been engaged by Christmas, fulfilling their destiny was no longer as important as the rest of their journey.

* * * * *

Get 4 FREE REWARDS!

We'll send you 2 FREE Books plus 2 FREE Mystery Gifts.

FREE
Value Over
$20

Both the **Harlequin® Special Edition** and **Harlequin® Heartwarming™** series feature compelling novels filled with stories of love and strength where the bonds of friendship, family and community unite.

YES! Please send me 2 FREE novels from the Harlequin Special Edition or Harlequin Heartwarming series and my 2 FREE gifts (gifts are worth about $10 retail). After receiving them, if I don't wish to receive any more books, I can return the shipping statement marked "cancel." If I don't cancel, I will receive 6 brand-new Harlequin Special Edition books every month and be billed just $5.24 each in the U.S. or $5.99 each in Canada, a savings of at least 13% off the cover price or 4 brand-new Harlequin Heartwarming Larger-Print books every month and be billed just $5.99 each in the U.S. or $6.49 each in Canada, a savings of at least 20% off the cover price. It's quite a bargain! Shipping and handling is just 50¢ per book in the U.S. and $1.25 per book in Canada.* I understand that accepting the 2 free books and gifts places me under no obligation to buy anything. I can always return a shipment and cancel at any time by calling the number below. The free books and gifts are mine to keep no matter what I decide.

Choose one: ☐ **Harlequin Special Edition**
(235/335 HDN GRCQ)

☐ **Harlequin Heartwarming**
Larger-Print
(161/361 HDN GRC3)

Name (please print)

Address   Apt. #

City   State/Province   Zip/Postal Code

Email: Please check this box ☐ if you would like to receive newsletters and promotional emails from Harlequin Enterprises ULC and its affiliates. You can unsubscribe anytime.

Mail to the Harlequin Reader Service:
IN U.S.A.: P.O. Box 1341, Buffalo, NY 14240-8531
IN CANADA: P.O. Box 603, Fort Erie, Ontario L2A 5X3

Want to try 2 free books from another series? Call 1-800-873-8635 or visit www.ReaderService.com.

HSEHW22R2

Get 4 FREE REWARDS!

We'll send you 2 FREE Books plus 2 FREE Mystery Gifts.

FREE Value Over **$20**

Both the **Harlequin® Historical** and **Harlequin® Romance** series feature compelling novels filled with emotion and simmering romance.

Get 4 FREE REWARDS!

We'll send you 2 FREE Books plus 2 FREE Mystery Gifts.

FREE
Value Over
$20

Both the **Romance** and **Suspense** collections feature compelling novels written by many of today's bestselling authors.

HARLEQUIN
PLUS

Announcing a **BRAND-NEW** multimedia subscription service for romance fans like you!

Read, Watch and Play.

Experience the easiest way to get the romance content you crave.

Start your **FREE 7 DAY TRIAL** at www.harlequinplus.com/freetrial.